BRISTOL CITY COUNCIL
LIBRARY SERVICES
WITHDRAWN AND OFFERED FOR SALE
SOLD AS SEEN

4 1 0260394 3

100 Golden Eagles for Iron Eyes

Bounty hunter Iron Eyes is heading south to Mexico in search of outlaws Bodine and Walters, but is himself being hunted down by his erstwhile sweetheart Squirrel Sally. Then Iron Eyes learns that Sally has been kidnapped by landowner Don Jose Fernandez, and rushes to her aid. But Sally, Iron Eyes and the outlaws are all just pawns in a much larger game, with an enemy more deadly than they can imagine, and Iron Eyes has to use all his courage and skill to survive.

By the same author

The Hunt for Iron Eyes
My Name is Iron Eyes
The Tomb of Iron Eyes
The Gun Master
A Noose for Iron Eyes
Fortress Iron Eyes

100 Golden Eagles for Iron Eyes

Rory Black

A Black Horse Western

ROBERT HALE

© Rory Black 2016
First published in Great Britain 2016

ISBN 978-0-7198-2042-7

The Crowood Press
The Stable Block
Crowood Lane
Ramsbury
Marlborough
Wiltshire SN8 2HR

www.crowood.com

Robert Hale is an imprint
of The Crowood Press

The right of Rory Black to be identified as
author of this work has been asserted by him
in accordance with the Copyright, Designs and
Patents Act 1988

Typeset by
Derek Doyle & Associates, Shaw Heath
Printed and bound in Great Britain by
CPI Group (UK) Ltd, Croydon, CR0 4YY

Dedicated to Gary and Karen George

PROLOGUE

The stagecoach rattled like the bones of a dozen skeletons as the feisty young female lashed her long leathers across the backs of the lathered-up team of horses below her perilous perch. Although Squirrel Sally was not familiar with either the replacement team of six black horses or the trail weary vehicle beneath her torn britches, she expertly steered the horses and creaking vehicle fearlessly. For young, head-strong girls like Sally Cooke could never be deterred from their chosen goals, no matter how many obstacles were cast in their path.

A mere ten days earlier she had ensured that Iron Eyes had kept his promise and purchased the stage-coach for her out of his reward money. Her original mode of transport had lost an argument with a fast moving waterfall and rocks. The notorious bounty hunter reluctantly used the bulk of his reward money and did as the unshakeable female had said.

Yet no sooner had she been gifted the battered old stagecoach than the notorious hunter of men had once again fled from her clutches in case she became too grateful.

Most young women might have taken the hint that perhaps Iron Eyes did not feel the same way toward her as she did for him. Most females, but not dead-shot Squirrel Sally.

Sally had other plans for her betrothed and no matter how many times he managed to slip away from her, she forgave him and doggedly trailed him. Like most besotted young ladies with their sights on her man, Sally was determined to get him.

It never seemed to matter to her how many times Iron Eyes mounted his tall stallion and spurred, for she always had an excuse for his actions. Nothing could stop her and she actually believed that the deadly bounty hunter was warming to her feminine charms.

In truth Iron Eyes was frightened of her. There seemed to be no reason why anything as young and pretty as Sally was to be infatuated by something that looked like he did. He had long been known as the living ghost due to his brutalized face and skeletal form. His features bore evidence of every battle he had ever waged.

Why would she want him when there were so many unscathed young men to choose from? He constantly wondered.

It did not make any sense.

He would willingly face heavily-armed outlaws without flinching but when it came to the fairer sex, the bounty hunter simply did not understand them.

Females of any description had always troubled the legendary bounty hunter. Squirrel Sally troubled him more than most. Another unspoken reason for him trying to leave Sally behind him was that he was worried that simply being near him was suicidal for anyone.

But against all the odds, the young female had saved his bacon on several occasions by her uncanny ability with her Winchester. Squirrel Sally had fought beside him better than most able-bodied men could ever have done and yet she was still a total mystery to Iron Eyes.

Why wouldn't she take the easy option and simply settle down in a safe place? Why did she choose to risk her neck and trail Iron Eyes into the most dangerous of places? Time and time again he had attempted to leave her somewhere safe but she had followed him.

Once again he had abandoned her and ridden out with fresh Wanted posters in his deep trail coat pockets but with her expert tracking skills, Sally had set out after him. The dust hung in the moonlight as the stagecoach hurtled down the barren desert road. Just like the man she followed, Squirrel Sally had no idea where she was heading.

She lashed the hefty reins down on the backs of her new team of horses and drove on through the moonlit night in pursuit of the man she proclaimed she was besotted with.

As she spat the dust from her mouth, her tightened eyes stared out at the distant horizon. She could see the unmistakable sight of a town's lights. The amber glow lit up the desert like a score of fire-flies.

A knowing smile came to her beautiful young face.

'So that's where you're headed, you scrawny bastard,' Sally whispered to herself as the horses hurtled across the eerie ground. 'You thought you could slink away from little Squirrel but you can't. I'm coming, Iron Eyes. Coming to get you.'

The stagecoach rattled on.

ONE

There had been just enough time for the tall, thin bounty hunter to water and feed the magnificent palomino stallion in the tiny Mexican settlement before he had continued on his quest to capture the elusive outlaws he had trailed across the border. The faces of the small settlement's people watched as Iron Eyes consumed half a bottle of rye and then returned the cork to its neck. Their unblinking eyes had watched the pitifully lean man in the long, blood-stained trail coat as he moved around the tail of his mount and checked the stallion for injury.

With every step his sharp spurs rang out in the quiet array of almost identical dwellings. The setting sun had lavished a crimson hue on the stranger they fearfully watched from their hiding places. None of them had ever seen anything quite like it before. For the fiery rays of the setting sun gave Iron Eyes the appearance of being aflame.

When satisfied that the stallion had eaten and drunk its fill, the fearless bounty hunter had known it was time to continue his deadly search.

It was only when Iron Eyes had pulled his long leathers free of a hitching pole and stepped back into a stirrup that they began to breathe again.

Then the solemn silence which had greeted the bounty hunter was broken by a rasping voice Iron Eyes recognized. He turned slowly with his long leathers in his bony grip and stared through the moonlight at the bulky frame of Hogan Defoe as he strode out from the cantina toward his oldest rival. Defoe was a bounty hunter like the pitifully gaunt man he railed against. Yet Defoe had even less morals than Iron Eyes and it showed.

'If it ain't my old pal, Iron Eyes,' he said as he paced out into the sand and then rested. The bulky man rested his knuckles on his hips and glared through his bushy eyebrows at the man he hated almost as much as the wanted outlaws he hunted. 'What brings you to these parts?'

Iron Eyes did not answer the question as he looped his long leathers around the hitching pole and then walked away from the handsome palomino.

'I asked you a damn question, scarecrow,' Defoe yelled.

Iron Eyes stopped and stood like a deathly vision.

12

The lantern light danced across the grips of his matched Navy Colts as they poked out from his flat stomach.

'You talking to me, Hogan?' he asked as he shook his long mane of black hair off his face and squinted at the troublesome man twenty feet from where he stood.

Defoe raised his left hand and jabbed angrily at the air between them. 'You're after Running Wolf, ain't you?'

The gaunt bounty hunter raised an eyebrow.

'I didn't even know that Injun was in these parts,' he answered as his long fingers flexed as they hovered in the air. 'I'm hunting different game.'

There seemed to be no reason why the far larger man was so angered by the sight of the infamous Iron Eyes, yet he was. His stumpy fingers poked at the air again as he squared up to his rival.

'You egg-sucking liar,' Defoe screamed. 'You can't fool me. I know you're after that rebel Injun and I'm gonna stop you from stealing my thunder. You always manage to steal my pickings from me but not this time. I'm gonna kill you this time, Iron Eyes.'

Iron Eyes narrowed his eyes. 'That'll be the day.'

There had never been any humour between the two bounty hunters and Iron Eyes had always managed to get the better of his far slower rival when it came to catching up to outlaws and killing them. It seemed that their brief and bloody encounters had weighed heavily on the muscular bounty hunter and this time he intended removing his competitor from his path.

'I'm gonna kill you, you stinking runt,' he vowed as his massive hand hovered above his holstered six-shooter. 'This is the last time you'll best me.'

Iron Eyes watched to see how far Defoe would go this time. He remained perfectly still as his disgruntled rival began to stride across the moonlit sand toward him.

'Let's see how fast you really are with them hog-legs of yours, you ugly bastard,' Defoe growled as he grabbed the grip of his .45 and hauled it from its holster. 'Go for them guns or I'll kill you where you stand.'

It did not require a second warning for Iron Eyes to drag his guns from behind his belt buckle. As Defoe swung his large frame around and went to fan his gun hammer with the palm of his left hand, the sound of the deadly Navy Colts rang out.

Two blinding flashes of venom burst from his gun barrels as the deafening sound of the matched guns echoed all around the whitewashed adobes.

Hogan Defoe had never been shot before but recognized the impact of the two bullets which knocked him backwards. His gloved hand fanned the hammer of his Peacemaker as he felt his knees buckle. The huge bounty hunter fell to his knees in shock as the gun fell from his hand. His hooded eyes glanced at

14

his opponent in surprise.

The sight of Iron Eyes holding his weapons as smoke trailed from their barrels baffled the large man as he rocked on his knees.

'You beat me to the draw,' he mumbled.

'And I killed you, Hogan.' Iron Eyes shook his head and pushed his smoking guns back into his waist band.

Defoe leaned back and stared at the tall emaciated figure before him. He was about to scream back at Iron Eyes when he noticed the two holes in his shirt front. Then blood began to pour through the damaged cotton bib and trail down over his rotund guts.

Iron Eyes watched as Defoe rolled on to his side.

'I told you that I'd killed you, Hogan,' he said as the last tune of Defoe's deathly rattle escaped from his stricken body. 'I told you that I weren't hunting Running Wolf. I'm after Brook Bodine and Shep Walters.'

Iron Eyes kicked the body over on to its back. The startled expression was one he had seen many times before. He turned and walked back to his horse.

'Reckon that dumb varmint won't be bothering me none anymore.' He spat angrily at the ground. 'I hate wasting lead on bastards who ain't worth nothing.'

His long fingers reached down, tugged the reins free of the hitching rail and looked around the street. The sound of music had ceased coming from the cantina as soon as the gunfire had rung out.

Iron Eyes grabbed the silver horn of his saddle, pushed his left mule-eared boot into his stirrup and pulled his thin frame off the ground. He looped his long right leg over the saddle and then gathered up the loose leathers. He turned the stallion away from the cantina and jabbed his sharp spurs into the flesh of the high shouldered animal.

As the palomino made its way between the cantina and another less imposing building, the sound of guitars rang out once more.

The sight of the unholy vision leaving the midst of the remote desert town filled every man, woman and child with a sense of relief. For even deep in the heart of the Mexican countryside they had all heard the stories of the gruesome figure who was reputed to be a living ghost and impossible to kill. After setting eyes upon the horrifically mutilated Iron Eyes, none of them doubted the fact.

The lifeless carcass left in his wake only confirmed the fact that Iron Eyes was no ordinary man. He had ended the existence of Hogan Defoe in the same manner that most men swatted an annoying fly.

Defoe had bugged his rival once too often and paid the ultimate price for doing so. As the sound of the stallion's pounding hoofs grew fainter the people of the small village emerged from their hiding places.

Like locusts they quickly stripped the bulky bounty hunter of his every possession and then fed his bloody corpse to their hogs.

TWO

Before the deadly gunfight, Iron Eyes had purchased feed for his mount and hard liquor and cigars for himself. He filled his empty canteens from the town's only source of water and hung them from the horn of his ornate saddle.

Yet the gaunt stranger had sensed that the quiet settlement was far more dangerous than it appeared at first sight. Something deep within his soul told him that trouble was brewing even though it was not what he had expected. The notorious bounty hunter had thought that maybe he had finally managed to catch up with the pair of wanted outlaws he sought.

He had not expected the brutal Defoe to be the one to appear from the shadows and force him to demonstrate his prowess with his deadly Navy Colts.

As the night air lifted his long hair off his scarred

face, Iron Eyes spurred on after the outlaws he still sought. After a few miles Iron Eyes noticed that there was a strange scent on the warm evening breeze. It was one he did not recognize.

The vast Pacific Ocean was far closer than the bounty hunter imagined. As one who had never even seen an ocean before, the strange aroma was confusing.

The further he rode, the stronger it became.

Dust flew up from the hoofs of his mount as he drove on deeper into the desert. His bullet coloured eyes stared at the marks left in the sand as he urged his palomino on. Iron Eyes doggedly followed the hoof tracks of his prey still clearly visible beneath the bright moon.

Soon Bodine and Walters would be in his gun sights.

The two outlaws had no sense of urgency in their spurs as they galloped up a sandy rise and looked back at the dusty desert behind the tails of their mounts. Brook Bodine pulled his reins up to his chest and looked back through the eerie moonlight at the relentless bounty hunter who had been trailing them since before they crossed the border. His partner swung his lathered-up horse around and looked to his cohort.

'Do you see him, Brook?' he asked as he struggled to keep his mount in check.

Bodine gave a nod of his head. 'I see him OK.'

Walters drew his horse close to his equally ruthless partner and peered through the strange light. They could both see the haunting horseman thundering after the trail they had carefully left in their wake.

A cruel smile filled Walters's face.

'That bounty hunter's real dumb, Brook.' He chuckled before swinging the horse around. 'I thought that he was said to be smart. He sure is an easy fish to hook.'

'Iron Eyes ain't dumb,' Bodine argued. 'He might be ugly and deadlier than a wounded mountain lion but he sure ain't dumb.'

Walters shrugged. 'He sure follows easy enough, though.'

'That's coz he reckons on killing us for the reward money and ain't even thought about us leading him on a wild goose chase.' Bodine pulled his tobacco pouch from his shirt pocket and started making a cigarette as his eyes continued to watch the dust rise from the palomino as it closed the distance on them. 'He ain't figured on us being paid to bring his sorrowful hide down here.'

'I sure hope we done the right thing.'

Bodine dried the sweat from his blistered face and turned his horse around. He ran his tongue along the gummed edge of the paper and then rolled the cigarette into shape. He poked it into the corner of his mouth and then fumbled in his vest pocket and

20

glanced at the crude instructions written upon a scrap of paper.

'It says that we gotta ride straight on,' the outlaw said through a cloud of smoke. 'Everything will be waiting for us when we reach the beach.'

'What if it ain't waiting for us?' the anxious Walters asked. 'We're dead men if it ain't.'

'Quit fretting, Shep,' Bodine said before sliding the paper back into his vest pocket and pulling out a match and scratching it with his thumbnail. He cupped the faltering flame and lit the tip of the cigarette. 'Everything will be fine. There'll be a boat waiting for us.'

'I sure hope you're right.'

'You and me both, Shep.' Bodine gulped as his eyes focused on the determined rider coming across the desert after them. 'I don't hanker for running out of sand and finding out we've bin tricked.'

Walters looked at his partner and swallowed hard. 'We'd better ride, Brook. That varmint is getting too damn close.'

Bodine filled his lungs with smoke and then tossed the spent cigarette at the ground. He glanced back at the awesome sight and then leaned over the neck of his exhausted horse.

'C'mon, pard,' he said, gripping his long leathers in his hands and nodding. 'You're right. That critter is getting too damn close.'

The outlaws spurred and rode on into the

21

moonlight. Dust hung in the evening gloom as both horsemen mercilessly drove their horses toward the distant ocean.

THREE

The bright moon and countless stars hung over the sandy terrain like a vulture awaiting its next meal to die. A cloud of dust surrounded the moon as the stagecoach continued on toward the small town that the infamous Iron Eyes had visited a few hours earlier. Yet not realizing that she had travelled deep into Mexico as she followed the bounty hunter, Sally was confused by what faced her.

Bathed in the eerie light of the brilliant moon, the town was unlike anything Squirrel Sally had ever seen before and that troubled the feisty girl.

Reaching down into the driver's well, she lifted a bottle of whiskey and eased its cork from the neck. She took a long swallow and then returned the stopper before dropping the clear glass vessel back down beside her Winchester.

The whiskey burned a trail down into her belly as its fumes cleared her tired head. Yet no matter how hard her beautiful eyes stared at the array of build-ings, they made no sense to her. The only towns Sally had ever seen before were constructed from red brick and wood and looked nothing like those before her.

'This ain't like no other town I've ever set eyes upon before,' Sally grumbled as she carefully rested her naked right foot on the brake pole. 'Ain't like nothing I knows about.'

The sight of whitewashed adobes surprised the young female as she eased back on the heavy reins and slowed the six-horse team down to a walk. Sally shook her long, dust-covered hair and stared harder at the town that faced her.

Just a dozen or so whitewashed adobes.

'Now this ain't normal,' she said to herself as she pushed her corn cob pipe into the corner of her mouth and lit its bowl with a match from her torn shirt. Smoke drifted from her perfect set of teeth as she tried to work out why every building was utterly different to anything she had ever seen before.

Even the moonlight could not disguise the fact that they were all white. She raised her eyebrows until they nearly vanished under her dust-caked golden locks.

The stagecoach rattled as its chains swayed in between the traces and the exhausted horses contin-ued on toward the small town.

Sally puffed on her pipe like a freight train as she

leaned back on the driver's seat and studied the buildings before her. To someone who had never been this far south before, the sight of anything apart from hastily constructed mining and cattle towns totally confused her. Even as the snorting team of horses headed into the solitary street, it still had not dawned on her that the trail of Iron Eyes had led her south of the border and deep into Mexico.

Mexico to Squirrel Sally was merely a name. As a girl who had never ventured off her parents' small farm until eleven months earlier, this was totally alien.

'Where in tarnation has that skinny galoot led me this time?' she wondered under her breath. 'This place ain't even American by the looks of it.'

She kept puffing on her pipe stem until the small bowl had extinguished its ration of tobacco. Her small hand pushed her unkempt golden hair off her face as she glanced around the array of lights which spilled from various windows and open doorways.

Without even thinking, Squirrel Sally drew up the rifle from the driver's box, cranked its mechanism and laid it across her lap. Even though she had not seen anyone yet, she could hear them. Guitars and joyful voices came washing over the sandy street before the hoofs of her lead horses.

The voices and music were also different to anything her cloistered mind had ever heard before. No matter how hard she tried, Sally could not understand anything the singing voices were happily uttering.

'What kinda lingo is that?' She sighed.

Sally pushed her pipe back into her pants pocket and stared from her high vantage point. She watched as the beaded curtain swayed in the evening breeze from the building where the activity was emanating from. Most of the town's folks were holed up inside, she guessed.

'That's gotta be some kind of saloon,' Sally told herself.

A few saddle horses were tied up at various points along the thoroughfare but there was no sign of their masters. Sally curled her index finger around the rifle trigger and allowed the team to keep walking toward the noisy structure.

'Where the heck am I?' she wondered. 'This sure ain't like no place I've ever bin before.'

As the stagecoach approached the noisy adobe, she pressed the brake pole harder and eased back on the reins. The horses stopped and then to her utter surprise a tall figure emerged from the shadows and stood before the lead horses.

He looked up at the unusual sight of a tiny attractive female in torn, revealing trail garb and smiled. He pointed at the cantina behind his back.

'This is a place to drink and eat, *señorita*,' he said in a deep Mexican accent.

Surprised, Sally frowned at the tall figure as he moved out of the shadows and stood before the swaying beads as the cantina's warm light cascaded over him.

She swung the Winchester and aimed its barrel at him.

The figure was unafraid. He grinned. His teeth caught the moonlight and gleamed at her.

'Do not shoot,' he said laughingly. 'I am not your enemy.'

'I don't know what you are, fella.' Sally frowned even harder and she kept the rifle aimed at the smiling man. 'All I know is that you got mighty good hearing and you don't seem to care for living.'

He was clad in a well-fitting outfit. A short jacket with silver thread detailing and a white frilly shirt drew her attention. A shining pistol holstered across his middle gleamed in the evening light.

'I care for living, *señorita*,' the figure informed her. 'I do not understand why you are so hostile to me.'

'Who is you exactly?' she snorted.

He walked along the line of horses. She kept the rifle on his every step.

'My name is Pablo,' he answered and stopped below her high seat. There was no hint of his being worried by the deadly rifle that was still perfectly aimed at him. 'And who are you, my beautiful one?'

Most men did not tend to act the way Pablo did when Sally aimed her Winchester at them. Normally they started to stammer and raise their hands above their heads. She could not understand

27

why this particular man was just grinning.

'Don't go making no sudden moves, Pablo,' Squirrel Sally said in her deepest voice. 'I'd hate to blow that pretty head off your shoulders.'

He shrugged and looked along the rifle barrel into her eyes and sighed.

'I have told you my name. Is your name a secret, pretty lady?' Pablo asked again from behind a disarming smile. 'What are you called?'

Totally surprised by his refusal to acknowledge the deadly rifle trained on his every movement, Sally leaned back and stared straight at him. Her temper was starting to boil as he continued to smile at her.

'My name's Sally.' She snorted furiously. 'Folks call me Squirrel Sally. Happy now?'

His brows lifted. 'That is a very unusual name.'

Sally lifted the rifle until its stock rested against her shoulder. 'You gonna make fun of my handle? Are you, huh?'

He shook his head. 'When a pretty girl has a pretty rifle aimed at me, I would never dare to make fun. Besides, I like your name. It is most attractive.'

'It is?' Sally looked bemused.

'Very seductive.' Pablo sighed.

'Good.' She gave a firm nod of her head. Her long golden hair whipped forward, sending a cloud of trail dust flying over the edge of the driver's seat. 'That means you'll live a while longer. If there's one thing I can't stand it's being made fun of by men who

28

are handsomer than me.'

Pablo rested his hands on the edge of the high driver's seat and bolstered himself up by using the small wheel below Sally's high perch.

'I am not handsomer than you, Squirrel,' he cooed like a lovesick turtle dove. 'You are a goddess in this mockery of a town. A beautiful angel sent from heaven to melt the souls of weaklings like myself.'

Sally could not help but lower the rifle as she felt the unusual redness of her cheeks wallow in his flattering words as they washed over her.

'You sure talk pretty, Pablo.' She sighed.

He stretched his every fibre until his lips were only inches from hers. His eyes burned into her eyes as his fingertips touched her moonlit mane of curls.

'I have never before seen a beautiful female like you, Squirrel,' Pablo said softly as he watched her close her eyes.

Then before she could do anything, he grabbed her rifle and tore it from her hands. He tossed the Winchester over his shoulder, grabbed her hair and hauled her brutally from the driver's seat.

She flew over his shoulder.

Squirrel Sally somersaulted in mid air and fell helplessly toward the sand. Luckily for the youngster, the churned up sand was soft as she landed heavily upon it. A cloud of dust erupted from all around her shapely form as she collided with the ground and landed on her back. Every ounce of wind was forced from the stunned female.

Normally Sally would have cussed the hind leg off a blue nosed donkey but it was all she could do just to lie on the sand and count the stars which filled her eyes.

Sally coughed and felt a draft rising up between her thighs. Her dazed mind told her that her britches had split again but it was pointless getting too worked up about it. She had bigger problems to fret about. She raised her head off the sand and watched as the handsome Mexican stepped back down off the stagecoach wheel and approach her with his pistol drawn and aimed at her.

Sally turned her head in search of her trusty Winchester. She had no sooner spotted the deadly carbine when she suddenly noticed two much larger men appear from the shadows to either side of the still smiling Pablo. One of the men picked her rifle up as the other remained just behind Pablo's left shoulder.

Snorting like a tormented bull, she got up on to her elbows and glared at them.

'Hell, Pablo,' Sally groaned indignantly. 'What in tarnation did you wanna go doing that for? I might have bust something.'

He tilted his head and looked down at her torn clothing and smiled at her.

'It appears that you have bust something,

Squirrel.' Pablo pointed the barrel of his nickel-plated pistol at her ripped pants and shirt.

Sally glanced down her prostrate form and realized that her britches were in far worse shape than she had first imagined. Her knees closed together as she blew her wavy locks off her face.

'I don't know where I am but I sure don't cotton to the way you treat folks around here,' she snarled. 'Don't you know who I am, fella? I'm betrothed to Iron Eyes. Him and me are bounty hunters and we kill critters like you just for the fun of it.'

Pablo nodded. 'I have heard of Iron Eyes and I have also heard of his woman. It is said that he is never too far from you, *señorita*.'

Sally smiled up at Pablo.

'Damn right,' she confirmed. 'That ugly bastard gets mighty ornery if some fancy dude like you even looks at me for too long. If I was you I'd skedaddle while you still can. He'll be mighty riled when he learns what you done to me.'

'This is good.' Pablo grinned. 'We want Iron Eyes to learn of this. We want him to be angry. Angrier than he has ever been before.'

Squirrel Sally looked totally baffled. 'You must be darn tired of living, Pablo. Iron Eyes ain't known for his sense of humour.'

Pablo Fernandez stepped forward until he hovered over her in the spilled light of the cantina. He was no longer smiling as he glared down at her.

He snapped his fingers at his *vaqueros.*

'Pick the pretty Squirrel up, Luis,' he commanded the muscular man behind his shoulders. 'Pick her up and secure her. We have got what we came to get. Now we shall take her back to the hacienda.'

Sally wanted to protest but every scrap of her normally limitless strength had escaped her. The large hands of Pablo's henchmen dragged her off the dusty ground and threw her against the side of the stagecoach. Before she could fall limply back to the ground she felt a powerful hand press her against the vehicle's door. The pressure of the hand that rested in the small of her back was so great she could feel her breasts being crushed.

'Take it easy, you big galoot,' Sally vainly protested. 'My chests are getting flattened here.'

Her protests fell on deaf ears. Within seconds her wrists were pulled back behind her back and secured with rawhide laces. She winced as the bonds were tightened. Sally glanced over her slim shoulder at Pablo.

'What the hell's going on here, Pablo?' she shouted as his underlings continued to manhandle her. 'You seem to want to die and I promise you that's what'll happen when Iron Eyes finds out about this.'

Pablo loosened the drawstring under his chin and then pulled his sombrero off his back and placed it on his head. He tilted his head and looked into her eyes.

'Your betrothed is a very difficult man to do business with, little Squirrel.' He smiled. 'The only way to
do so is to lure him here. You are the bait, my pretty
one.'

It suddenly dawned on Sally that she was part of
some devilish plan the grinning man had conceived.

'You want Iron Eyes to come after me, don't you?'
she said fearfully. 'You want my man to ride into your
guns. You're gonna try and kill Iron Eyes.'

Pablo did not answer. He snapped his fingers
again and both his men obeyed the command.

They lifted Sally off her bare feet as if she weighed
little more than a feather. The coach door was
opened and she was thrown into the interior of the
vehicle. The burly men lashed the doors with an
uncoiled saddle rope so that it was impossible for her
to escape.

Sally rested against the padded seats and stared at
the door as the tall figure of Pablo Fernandez looked
in at his captured prey.

'You can't be serious, can you?' Sally yelled.
'Nobody ever gets the better of Iron Eyes. Let me go
and I won't tell him what you done to me. You'll be
six feet under if'n you don't.'

Pablo did not answer his captive. He signalled to
both his *vaqueros*. One climbed up on to the driver's
seat with her rifle as the other went to the side of the
whitewashed cantina and led their three horses
toward the stationary vehicle.

33

As the amber light cascaded across the moonlit sand, Pablo mounted his tall thoroughbred and watched as one of their horses was tethered to the tailgate of the stagecoach. He signalled to the man above him.

'Take the stagecoach to my father's hacienda, Raul.' He gestured as he controlled his eager mount. 'Luis and I shall follow after we have completed the second part of my father's plan.'

'*Sí*, Pablo.' The man thrashed the heavy leathers down across the backs of the team. The six horses pulled away from the cantina and headed out into the darkness.

Pablo turned his horse and nodded to Luis.

'Our business here is done, my friend,' he said as the burly Luis mounted his horse. 'Now we have to inform the famous Iron Eyes that my father wishes to speak with him.'

Luis gathered up his reins and stared at his boss.

'But what if this Iron Eyes does not want to speak with Don Jose, Pablo?'

Pablo placed a cigar between his teeth and then struck a match. He raised the flame to the long black length of tobacco and inhaled the flavoursome smoke.

'Do not worry. Iron Eyes will speak with my father when he learns that we have his woman, Luis,' he said through a cloud of smoke.

Luis looked concerned. 'But Iron Eyes is not like

34

other men, Pablo. They say that he shoots first and asks questions afterwards. The fact that we have his woman might just make him angrier than he usually is said to be.'

Pablo considered the problem. 'I have heard that his face is terribly scarred, Luis. Men who look more like monsters than real men tend to look after their women. He is lucky to have such a beautiful little *señorita* and I think he must know this. He will not give us any trouble.'

Luis crossed his chest in prayer. 'I hope you are right, Pablo.'

Pablo Fernandez adjusted his drawstring under his chin.

'So do I, *amigo.*' He sighed.

The large *vaquero* nodded as he turned his mount. 'Where will we find this deadly bounty hunter, Pablo?'

'Iron Eyes has been followed ever since he crossed the border, *amigo*. My father's spies have told me exactly where he can be found, Luis,' Pablo explained as he tapped his spurs into the flesh of his horse and headed west. 'He is in Costa Angelo.'

As Luis rode alongside Pablo, he adjusted his sombrero until its wide brim rested in the furrows of his brow.

'If this Iron Eyes is so ugly how can such a pretty girl like the golden-haired one in the coach be in love with him, Pablo?' he asked.

'Love is blind, my big friend,' Pablo replied. 'Love is truly blind.'

As the two horsemen thundered across the moonlit sand in the direction of Costa Angelo, they could still hear the loud vocals coming from the stagecoach as it headed off toward the hacienda of Don Jose Fernandez.

FOUR

The scent of the warm Pacific waters lapping against the Mexican beach alerted the dishevelled bounty hunter that the trail he had doggedly followed for the previous five days and nights was coming to an end. Iron Eyes raised his brutalized face and stared out through the darkness at the shoreline. The light of stars and the large moon rippled toward the shore as the sturdy palomino walked across the sand toward it.

As his high-shouldered stallion headed down from the moonlit slope toward the water, it was clear to Iron Eyes that his prey had flown. Two sets of hoof tracks led right up to the water and mysteriously disappeared in the waves.

It seemed impossible to Iron Eyes but the tracks led to a place where he knew no rider would go. To ride into the ocean was suicidal and the gaunt horseman knew that Bodine and Walters were many things but they were not suicidal.

This had to be a trick, he told himself.

It appeared that both outlaws had vanished into the waves like phantoms. But Iron Eyes did not believe in phantoms. This was a trick.

A cunning ploy designed to throw him off their trail. The longer he stared at the ocean, the more he began to believe that they might have just succeeded.

A good horse could carry a rider across a swollen river without too much trouble but rivers are not tidal like oceans. Rivers have banks on both sides that are usually visible. Not even a loco bean would dare to try and cross anything as wide as this.

It seemed that he had lost his chance of getting his bony hands on the $3,000 reward money and was riled. For the first time he had failed to ensnare the wanted men he had pursued and could not understand how.

Iron Eyes drew back on his reins and stopped the powerful animal beneath his highly decorated saddle. He steadied the animal and stared at the hoof marks which led to the ocean and disappeared in the incoming tide before him.

He wanted to draw his Navy Colts and empty every bullet in their chambers into the lapping waves that continued to mock him but even the infamous bounty hunter knew he could not kill a whole ocean.

'Damn it all,' he growled angrily and beat his fist on the silver horn of his saddle. 'Nobody ever gets away from Iron Eyes.'

His fiery eyes narrowed. He was fuming with rage.

'This just can't be.' Iron Eyes snorted in frustra-
tion. 'Them outlaws ain't smart enough to get the
better of me.'

His skeletal hand reached back, lifted the flap of
one of his saddle bag satchels and pulled out the last
of his whiskey bottles. Without looking at the bottle
he raised it to his savaged lips. His sharp teeth
gripped the cork and pulled it free of the bottle
neck.

Whiskey fumes filled his flared nostrils.

'How the hell did they do this?' he wondered. 'It
just ain't possible.'

The hard liquor burned a trail down his dry throat
as he kept staring at the vast expanse of water.

It just did not make any sense.

The bright moon cast its unearthly illumination
across the vast ocean as he vainly searched for a
glimpse of the two horsemen who seemingly had
ridden into it.

Iron Eyes threw the cork at the sand and then
raised the bottle to his scarred lips again. He consumed every last drop of the fiery liquor and then
angrily flung the clear glass vessel into the waves.

Waves that defiantly kept on moving toward the
hoofs of his handsome horse. If the two outlaws
imagined that Iron Eyes would meekly accept defeat
and ride away, they were very much mistaken. This

was a puzzle. One which he was determined to solve. Iron Eyes threw his long right leg over the mane of the palomino and slid to the sand.

'You think I'm just gonna swallow this?' he snarled through gritted teeth. 'If you do, you're wrong. I'll figure this out even if it takes all night.'

The emaciated bounty hunter walked away from his mount to where the hoof tracks of the outlaws' horses disappeared into the water. He shook his head in disbelief as he tried to work out how they had achieved this illusion.

He knelt and studied the sand even more intently as the hoof tracks dissolved in the lapping water. After a few seconds he rose back to his full height and shook his head again. His bony fingers pushed his limp hair off his face as his mule-eared boots sank into the wet sand. Then something a hundred yards away caught his keen attention.

His eyes narrowed.

It looked like a black mound of coal but he knew that there was no coal in these parts. He inhaled deeply and caught the scent of death in his flared nostrils.

He grabbed the long leathers of his mount and proceeded along the beach toward it. With every step, the strange dark shapes became clearer. The closer he got the more the moonlight enlightened the object of his curiosity.

Then he could see clearly what it was.

The two dead saddle horses had almost been enveloped by the incoming tide. The waves were washing over the legs and bellies of the stricken animals as he dropped his reins and stepped over the first carcass.

His eyes darted between them.

Both dead horses were saddled. Their masters had left their expensive trimmings but they had taken both of the saddle bags. The bounty hunter leaned over and found the leather rifle scabbards. The Winchesters had been removed from them. Then he spotted the bullet holes in the side of the animals' heads.

Two clean wounds. These exhausted creatures had not been put out of their misery due to severe injury, they had been callously executed. Both horses had been shot dead and left to be washed away by the tide.

That must have been the outlaws' plan, Iron Eyes thought. To make him believe they had ridden into the waves. But he had arrived at the beach before the ocean had time to claim the horses' bodies.

All he was meant to find were only the hoof tracks that led into the sea, but he had travelled far faster than either Bodine or Walters had anticipated.

Iron Eyes straightened up. He was not so easily fooled as most of his profession.

He had driven the mighty stallion far harder than most men would ever dare push their mounts.

41

Surviving on rations of cigars and whiskey and going without sleep had gained a whole day on the outlaws.

Walters and Bodine had wrongly assumed that the bodies of the horses would be long gone before their relentless hunter reached the beach.

Iron Eyes made his way back to the palomino stallion. He paused and looked back at the carcasses as the waves crashed over them. Soon they would be dragged into the vast ocean and consumed.

Then they would be gone forever.

He grabbed his reins and tugged.

The large stallion followed its master as Iron Eyes walked back to where the hoof tracks were still visible. Iron Eyes halted. Something else had alerted his honed senses.

As his bullet coloured eyes looked up, he caught a glimpse of something standing close to the dune beside a fishing boat.

He dropped the reins and flexed his bony fingers. Iron Eyes watched the man through the limp strands of his long black hair as he steadily approached.

The large sombrero cast an unholy shadow in the moonlight.

So did the ammunition belts across his chest.

'So you are the stinking dog who has been following my *amigo*s,' the man stated as he rested the palms of his hands on his holstered guns.

Iron Eyes raised his head until his tortured features were fully exposed.

42

'Yep. I'm the stinking dog that's been trailing Bodine and Walters,' he hissed like a sidewinder in reply.

The Mexican gunman suddenly stopped advancing. The sight before him was both a surprise and a shock. He had never before set eyes on anything that came close to looking the way Iron Eyes looked.

'Who are you?' he stammered.

'I'm your executioner, *amigo*,' Iron Eyes said. 'I'm Iron Eyes.'

Even south of the border the name of the legendary bounty hunter was well known. Few actually believed the torrid tales connected to the name. Even fewer believed the description of Iron Eyes could be true but when their eyes set upon his savaged countenance, all doubts evaporated.

'Iron Eyes?' The man hesitated as he sensed his own demise getting close. 'You are Iron Eyes?'

The bounty hunter strode across the sand toward the shaking creature he took to be a bandit. Iron Eyes stopped less than ten feet from the heavily laden man. He had never seen so much ammunition on one man before.

'What do you know about this?' the bounty hunter snarled.

'Bodine paid me to wait and watch, *señor*,' the shaking creature answered. 'I was to make sure that the bounty hunter remained here.'

'And if I decided to ride away from here?' Iron

43

Eyes asked as his long skeletal fingers continued to move like spiders above the grips of his guns. 'Then what were you meant to do?'

The bandit gulped. He was not sure.

Iron Eyes sighed and nodded as his icy glare burned into the shaking man. 'You got bounty on you, stranger?'

The man forced a pathetic smile. '*Sí señor*. I am wanted dead or alive and worth 200 pesos. They call me Mexican Joe.'

'Well, Mexican Joe,' Iron Eyes started. 'Tell me where Bodine and Walters went.'

'I am sworn to secrecy, *señor*,' the bandit replied. 'Nothing you can do will make me tell you what you wish to know.'

'OK.' Iron Eyes dragged both his Navy Colts from his belt, cocked their hammers and then fired. Both bullets carved a route from the guns and tore into the wanted man.

The bandit flew backward and crashed in a bloody heap in the shade of the fishing boat. Iron Eyes strode over to the body and then pushed his still smoking weapons back behind his belt buckle.

'I'm sure glad you were wanted dead or alive, Joe.' Iron Eyes spat at the corpse and turned back to where his palomino stallion was standing. 'I plumb hate wasting lead on folks who ain't worth nothing.'

FIVE

Like a haunting statue, Iron Eyes stood beside the high-shouldered stallion and thought about the situation he had ridden into. What should have been a normal chase had turned into something quite different and the gaunt Iron Eyes did not like it one bit. He was tired from days of constant riding but knew that there would be no time to rest until he had slain both Walters and Bodine. Most bounty hunters would have considered trying to bring them in alive but not the intrepid Iron Eyes. He only hunted those who the law stated were unfit to live and killed them.

For some unknown reason the two outlaws had tried to make it appear that they had ridden into the vast Pacific in a bid to shake off whoever was hunting them.

Iron Eyes still could not understand the motive behind the attempted deception. Only a fool would fall for that, he told himself.

Were they trying to make it appear that they had committed suicide? Was that it? Did they have some plan that required that they kill their mounts and simply vanish? None of it made any sense to the cold-hearted bounty hunter.

Were they so afraid of him they would risk the waves?

Were they willing to risk death just to avoid facing the wrath of the legendary Iron Eyes?

To Iron Eyes death was a constant companion and nothing to be feared. He had learned that lesson when he had first set traps in order to fill his belly. Death was always far closer than anyone could imagine. Always waiting on the one mistake we all eventually make.

The Grim Reaper took no prisoners.

Neither did Iron Eyes.

So why had the outlaws tried to make him believe the unbelievable? The problem festered inside his skull as his eyes darted between the dead horses and the dead bandit.

Why had they hired the hapless Mexico Joe? Maybe Joe was meant to kill anyone who came looking for the outlaws. If Joe had managed to fulfil his contract he was probably meant to go and tell Bodine and Walters.

That meant that the outlaws would be coming ashore somewhere close, Iron Eyes reasoned. Somewhere very close indeed.

He stepped into the closest stirrup and hauled himself back up on to his Mexican saddle. His prized stallion remained alert as it waited for its master's next command. Iron Eyes looked at the waves and grinned.

'I sure hope you don't drown before I get a chance to kill you, boys,' he hissed and gathered up his long leathers.

The gaunt horseman turned the stallion and tapped his spurs. The palomino headed back toward the dunes. Iron Eyes noted that along the beach there were at least a half dozen other fishing boats resting beneath the bright moon. Their nets swayed in the gentle breeze.

Bodine and Walters were probably still out there on the shimmering waves somewhere, he thought. Iron Eyes did not envy the outlaws rowing a boat on the rolling waves.

The tall stallion passed the dead Mexican bandit who had made the mistake of facing the legendary bounty hunter and underestimating him. Iron Eyes touched his temple in silent salute and then searched the deep pockets of his trail coat for something to fuel his weary mind. The sound of loose bullets filled the night air as his long bony fingers located what he was looking for.

Iron Eyes withdrew his hand. He had plucked a long thin cigar from his deep coat pockets without breaking it. He rammed it between his scarred lips and gripped it with his razor sharp teeth. He pulled a match from his shirt pocket and ignited it with his thumbnail.

A golden glow lit up his hideous features as he cupped the fiery eruption against the ocean breeze.

The flickering flame was raised to the cigar. Iron Eyes sucked on the weed until his lungs were full of the acrid smoke and then he flicked the match at the sand.

He mercilessly pulled on his reins, turned the mighty stallion and looked around the ridge of dunes that faced the breaking waves. He had not observed anything on his determined ride to the beach. All his scarred eyes had seen were the hoof tracks which had led him to this place. Now it was time to study his surroundings more carefully.

Iron Eyes held the powerful horse in check as he spotted a line of colourful lanterns swinging in the sea breeze about a mile away from where he sat. Below the lanterns were amber lights spilling from numerous doors and windows.

There was a small fishing village almost hidden by the dunes. Iron Eyes exhaled a long line of smoke at his observances. It was just far enough along the beach for him to get a good view of the fishing boat should the outlaws decide to return to shore. He tapped his blood-stained spurs into the flanks of the stallion and got the huge palomino walking toward the sandy rise.

As the stallion obeyed its master's painful commands, Iron Eyes thought about the two outlaws and how he should kill them. It was usually his habit to kill wanted outlaws quickly but these men had tried to fool him. That angered the bounty hunter and he wanted to make them pay.

Nobody tricked Iron Eyes and lived to brag about it.

The skeletal horseman stood in his stirrups as the handsome animal climbed up the dunes. Iron Eyes sat back down and aimed his mount at the distant lights. Cigar smoke drifted over his wide shoulders as he encouraged the horse to find more pace.

Smoke billowed from between his teeth as Iron Eyes turned his brutalized head and looked back at the moonlit water. He did not envy anyone out on the incoming waves. He reasoned that the outlaws would not dare to take the boat out too far from the shore. Even deadly outlaws ought to have enough sense to figure out that ocean waves could be as lethal as his Navy Colts.

The sea did not take prisoners, either.

'They'll be real green by the time they set foot on dry land again, horse,' Iron Eyes snorted and slapped the neck of his mount. 'Killing them critters is just gonna be too damn easy.'

They would probably row the boat as best they could along the coastline to where they could come ashore safely, he deduced. If they did not capsize it

49

first. It was obvious that neither outlaw had worked out what they were going to do after they returned to dry land.

This was not Texas and there was not an abundant supply of horses to either buy or steal in these parts. Since crossing the unmarked border, Iron Eyes had seen a lot of oxen and burros but not one saddle horse. If Bodine and Walters had assumed that they could easily get their hands on fresh mounts, they were sadly mistaken.

Saddle horses were as rare as hen's teeth in these parts, he thought. Bodine and Walters would soon live to regret killing their precious horses down on the beach.

The outlaws might have shaken him off for now, Iron Eyes silently admitted, but no matter how long it took, he would wait for them to reappear. Then he would face their guns and kill them with his usual sadistic ease.

His hands eased back on his reins. The stallion slowed and started to walk through the eerie moonlight toward the colourful swaying lanterns. Iron Eyes carefully reloaded his Navy Colts as the palomino carried on walking.

Iron Eyes slid his primed six-shooters into his deep trail coat pockets next to the loose bullets in readiness for what he knew would soon happen as the high shouldered stallion steadily continued toward the small fishing village. When Bodine and Walters finally came back ashore they would be even more dangerous than the wanted posters implied.

That did not trouble the haunting rider, though.

Iron Eyes would be ready for them.

He gripped the long black cigar between his teeth and then caught the familiar aroma of cooking food in his flared nostrils. Iron Eyes knew there was plenty of time to eat before he had to face the outlaws. Time enough to fill his lean frame with the food he seldom allowed to pass his lips.

Iron Eyes tapped his spurs. It had been a long while since he had eaten anything. He was about ready to start again.

The palomino trotted on toward the swaying lanterns.

SIX

The elegant Don Jose Fernandez stood within the courtyard of his impressive hacienda like a general awaiting the return of his troops from battle. Yet there was no sense of victory in his aged soul. For Fernandez was not looking for trouble, only the solution to trouble that had unexpectedly sought him out.

The hacienda was at the heart of the land he and his family had owned for over a century. Yet for all his wealth none of this meant anything to the silver haired Fernandez.

He had a dozen *vaqueros* working for him, yet not one of them could do what he required doing. None of his men had the cunning or skills to achieve the seemingly impossible. He had sent out his only son with two of his best *vaqueros* to find the golden-haired Squirrel Sally and bring her back to the whitewashed hacienda.

Yet it was not the young female he wanted.

It was her man.

Bringing Squirrel Sally to his hacienda was a bid to entice the otherwise elusive Iron Eyes out of the shadows to where Don Jose wanted him. It was pointless trying to ask the bounty hunter to pay the remote hacienda a visit. Men like Iron Eyes would never respond to a normal request. They had to be hooked like a savage catfish and reeled in. To do that you needed the correct bait and Squirrel Sally was the only bait they knew could entice him to them.

A month earlier, Don Jose had sent his best *vaqueros* deep into Texas in search of Iron Eyes. Once located, they had to carefully make him start hunting Bodine and Walters.

Somehow they had managed to lure the bounty hunter away from his usual hunting grounds. They had done the seemingly impossible and got the bounty hunter to track the two outlaws deep into Mexico. Without knowing it, Iron Eyes was doing exactly what Don Jose Fernandez wanted him to do.

Iron Eyes was trailing Bodine and Walters back to the land Fernandez and his family ruled. It had been far easier getting Sally to bite at their bait and follow Iron Eyes.

Don Jose's *vaqueros* kept in constant touch with their employer until he knew exactly where the gaunt bounty hunter and his beautiful follower were.

Fernandez inhaled on his long slim cigar as his

men milled around the elegant household. The equally elegant Don Luis had been standing on his porch for hours as he waited in the moonlight for a sign that the operation was successful.

Then off in the distance amid an ocean of sand, he saw the eerie light of the moon catching the rising dust of a stagecoach as it came over a crest and began heading toward him.

Don Jose looked to the well-armed men in the courtyard of his splendid home.

'Prepare yourselves, *amigos*,' he called out to them. 'They are coming with the bait we need to bring Iron Eyes into our midst.'

SEVEN

The wheels of the stagecoach seemed to find every rut in the makeshift road as the burly *vaquero* lashed Sally's bullwhip above the heads of the exhausted team. There was an urgency in the hands of the driver as he forced the six horses on toward the moonlit hacienda.

With her hands tied behind her back, Squirrel Sally was tossed around the inside of the coach like a rag doll as it travelled along the moonlit road. The burly *vaquero* on the driver's seat lashed the long leathers down on the backs of the six-horse team as the vehicle thundered through the moon-light toward its mysterious destination. Then as the six powerful black horses veered to the left, the stagecoach was nearly upended and Sally found herself flipped up on to one of the padded benches.

The fearless female arched her tiny body against the back and side bulkheads of the coach. It took every ounce of her youthful strength and willpower to remain upon the soft seat as all four wheels returned to the ground.

Finally she had managed to remain in one spot long enough to look out of the vehicle's windows. The scenery was bathed in the strange blue light of the bright overhead moon as the stagecoach rocked on its leather springs. Sally inhaled deeply as she watched the barren terrain flash past the window she was pressed up against.

Wherever she was, it was totally unknown to her.

Clouds of dust were kicked up by the horse's hoofs and the stagecoach wheels. Sally squinted hard in a vain bid to try and work out where she was being taken but this land was unlike any other she had ever experienced before. The unfamiliar land-scape unfolded before her. The bright moon cast its unholy illumination across the desert but did nothing to explain to her young mind where she was headed.

Her dust-covered face could see something ahead as she poked her head out of the window. Two glowing torches a half mile ahead of the gal-loping team appeared to be set to either side of the road.

'Where in tarnation am I being taken?' Sally muttered as dust filled her mouth. She spat at the ground but refused to withdraw back into the stagecoach.

She was as curious as a six-legged cat and determined to learn the answers to the countless questions that buzzed inside her head.

The handsome Pablo had charmed her with his well-practised flattery and then managed to get the better of her. That seemed stupid to the bruised female.

Why had she been tossed into the coach of her stage? Did Pablo want her as well as her stagecoach?

Then her bruised head recalled the young Mexican telling her that she was merely the bait to entice Iron Eyes into his father's trap.

Sally swallowed hard. Was she going to be the downfall of the man she adored? Her heart pounded inside her ill-fitting shirt.

Buffeted like a bronco buster as the stagecoach thundered through the night, Sally frowned and raised her leg. She gripped the rope that had been used to ensure the carriage door could not be opened with her flexible toes.

Then she pressed her back against the padded backrest and steadied her small frame from being further thrown around the interior of the coach. She exhaled as her bottom bounced up and down on the padded seat.

Sally blew the loose strands of long golden hair off her face and shook her head.

'What the hell is going on here?' she muttered to herself as the glancing light of fiery torches filled the coach.

With the same curiosity that had killed countless cats, the beautiful dust-caked female slid across the seat and poked her head out of the window once more.

Dust blew into her face, adding to the already thick layer that still covered it. She spat and screwed her eyes up tightly.

Her face was peppered by grit and dust but Sally caught a brief glimpse of two beacons behind the stagecoach. Flames leapt up from the blazing torches set atop stone plinths and licked at the sky.

'Where the hell are you taking me, you fat galoot?' she screamed at the top of her voice as she shook the dust and debris from her mane of golden locks. 'Where are we?'

As she vainly tried to comprehend the motives behind her abduction, the coach suddenly rocked on its springs. The alert female knew that the stagecoach was being turned hard to the right.

'You better not hurt any of my team with that kinda driving,' Sally shouted. 'Turning horses that hard could make them bust a gut.'

Then out of the carriage window, her blue eyes spied a long structure set out in the eerily dark desert surrounded by high walls. Amber light glowed like a herd of fireflies amid the shadows like a lighthouse set in a sea of sand.

Although Squirrel Sally did not realize it, she was now being taken into the stronghold of one of Mexico's wealthiest families. The stagecoach was heading into the heart of the hacienda belonging to Don Jose Fernandez.

'What the hell is that doing out here in the middle of nowhere?' Sally mumbled as she fought to remain upright as the stagecoach took another severe turn.

Countless lanterns and torches guided the stage-coach toward it. The sound of chains rattling between the team's traces filled the interior of the coach as Squirrel Sally tried to get a better look at the magnificent edifice.

Then she saw riders. They had come from the whitewashed hacienda to escort the coach into the building's grounds. Sally could see the moonlight glint off their rifles and pistols.

A concerned expression filled her face.

Suddenly the reality of the situation began to dawn upon her. She watched as the horsemen rode beside both the carriage doors. The riders rested the stocks of their rifles on their thighs as they flanked the speeding stagecoach.

'This ain't good,' she muttered softly. 'This ain't good at all.'

As the inquisitive youngster moved her head back to the window of the rocking vehicle, it was driven back by the gleaming metal barrel of the rider's

Winchester. More dust and splinters filled the interior of the coach.

Sally stared up at the horseman with a look that could sour cream.

The hacienda grew even larger as the stagecoach closed in on it. Sally propelled herself across to the opposite bench and stared at the large whitewashed wall. There were men on the wall's parapets.

Men with rifles.

Her buttocks felt the slowing of the stage.

Sally braced herself by placing her bare feet on the opposite bench seat. She did not want to end on the floor of the coach again.

Finally, as the team was slowed, she heard the brake pole being engaged. The ear-piercing sound of the leather pads arguing with the wheel rims grated her senses.

'I'd better remember to grease them brakes,' Sally snorted as the stagecoach jolted to a halt. 'If I ever get a chance, that is.'

The stagecoach stopped. The light of numerous torches and lanterns filled the carriage as the rocking of the vehicle finally ebbed.

Sally strained to free her hands but the rawhide tethers would not give. She gritted her teeth and stared through her long hair at the carriage door.

Every fighting instinct in the feisty female wanted to tear into her captors when they opened the door of the coach but even a cougar could not pounce when its paws were tied behind its back.

For a few endless moments nothing happened.

Then as the dust finally settled, she saw the elegant face of Don Jose looking at her through the window as one of his men sliced through the rope that secured the door.

Fernandez opened the door and looked into the blazing eyes of Squirrel Sally. He had heard of the young girl who was said to be the mate of Iron Eyes. He had expected someone older and was surprised by the attractive female.

He gave a bow of his head.

'You are the famed Squirrel Sally?' he politely asked. 'The one who belongs to Iron Eyes?'

Sally blew a loose curl off her face and nodded.

'He belongs to me, more like,' she corrected.

'Please pardon my error.' Don Jose nodded. 'You are Squirrel Sally, though?'

'Damn right I am, old timer,' she growled as her feet rested on the floor of the carriage. 'And I'm gonna rip your heart out of your frilly shirted chest when I get a chance.'

'I understand your anger, *señorita*,' Don Jose said as he watched Sally disembark the vehicle. 'When you learn our reasons for bringing you here I hope you will look more kindly on me.'

'I surely doubt it,' Sally grunted as *vaqueros* held her in check and led her past the nobleman as she lashed out with her feet.

Fernandez stepped back and signalled with his hands to the *vaqueros* to either side of him.

'Take our guest to her room, amigos,' he said. 'But be careful. I think the little squirrel is as dangerous as her reputation implies.'

EIGHT

The warm sea breeze wafted over the moonlit beach and the assembly of whitewashed adobes which were strung along the top of the dunes. The magnificent palomino had attracted the attention of the small settlement's people, for as its owner had rightly calculated, horses were a rarity in this region.

Powerful thoroughbreds were even less common. Yet none of the curious ventured too close to the animal as it stood drinking its fill from a trough beside the exterior of the cantina.

The haunting stare which the bounty hunter flashed like a honed dagger had silently caused even the most curious of souls to eventually retreat and leave both horse and master in peace. For it was obvious to even the dullest of wits that Iron Eyes was not the sort of creature to rile. The threat of death oozed from his every pore in silent warning.

The bounty hunter watched the breaking waves

from the courtyard of the cantina. He was waiting for Bodine and Walters to row back to the beach like a cat waiting for birds to land. When they did, he would pounce.

The singing and guitar playing still spilled through the swaying beads but Iron Eyes did not listen to the joyous sound. His cold-blooded attention remained focused on the beach below the fishing village. Somewhere out there the outlaws were hiding in the rolling surf. When they came ashore, he would be waiting for them with his prized Navy Colts.

Methodically, Iron Eyes had forced down a bowl of strong chilli and mopped up its crimson gravy with a chunk of bread as his small unblinking eyes observed everyone and everything before him.

Nothing of importance would evade his icy stare as he sat alone beneath the large moon. The coloured lanterns swayed on the fine ropes that fringed the courtyard but they too went unnoticed by the single-minded avenger.

The sound of festivity from within the cantina still wafted through the beaded curtain but it meant nothing to the bounty hunter. All Iron Eyes was interested in was Bodine and Walters.

Once he killed them, he could ride back across the border and claim their bounty. It was as simple as that in his mind.

Iron Eyes dropped the spoon on the plate, wiped

his mouth on the back of his sleeve and pushed it into the middle of the circular table. His innards were not used to solid food and the sensation of the chilli filling his painfully thin guts was uncomfortable. He pushed a thumb into his belt and belched. The stallion raised its head from the trough and looked at the skeletal figure.

'You've made worse,' the bounty hunter sneered. The stallion returned its head back to the cool liquid.

Iron Eyes had positioned his lean frame so that he was sat at an angle which allowed him to watch the water line as he ate. If a boat was to suddenly wash up on the beach, he would spot it before anyone else in the tiny fishing village. Yet for nearly an hour Iron Eyes had not seen anything to warrant his brutal attention.

Sleep was a luxury that the bounty hunter had not allowed himself since he had set out after both deadly outlaws. No matter how weary he became, Iron Eyes refused to acknowledge it. Only lesser mortals slept when there was work to do, he continually told his tired mind.

The sound to his left told him that someone had moved through the dangling beads. Iron Eyes did not turn his head to try and see who because he already knew. He recognized the sound of her bare feet as they moved across the tiles toward him.

A well-proportioned female with long black hair tied in a pony tail had bravely faced her own fears and waited upon her unusual customer several times. She had brought him his food and the six bottles of tequila he had requested. A large golden eagle had paid for his order with plenty of unwanted change.

'Did you enjoy your supper, *señor*?' she managed to ask without allowing her eyes to linger upon her customer's face.

'It was fine,' Iron Eyes mumbled as he kept watching the breaking waves.

The female glanced at the beach and then back at Iron Eyes curiously. 'What are you looking at?'

'I'm waiting for a row boat to come ashore,' he whispered.

'But the men do not fish when the sun is down, *señor*,' she said to him. 'There will be no boats coming ashore.'

Iron Eyes sighed heavily. 'We'll see.'

No matter how deadly he appeared to be, he interested her in a way few of the locals had ever done. She stood close to the seated bounty hunter. 'What do they call you?'

'Who?'

'Your friends, *señor*.' She sighed heavily. Her ample bosom caught the rays of the moon and sparkled as sweat trickled over them. 'My name is Conchita. What do your friends call you?'

Iron Eyes frowned. The question made no sense. As far as he was concerned, he had no friends. Squirrel Sally was a pest that he could not seem to

66

shake off, but he had never thought of her as a friend.

'My name's Iron Eyes,' he muttered without looking at her.

'That is an unusual name.'

The buxom Conchita floated around the table and wondered how many more golden eagles this fearsome figure might have hidden in the depths of his blood-stained pockets.

To her, gringo money was always better than any-thing her own country ever minted. She had taken the golden coin and slipped it between her large breasts and allowed it to nestle in their warmth. There was plenty of room for more.

'You need the company of a woman tonight,' Conchita told him as she wandered around his motionless form. 'A good woman who will pleasure you. A woman like me.'

Iron Eyes rubbed his thumb along his jaw. 'I'm kinda busy, Conchita.'

It had only been a hundred heartbeats since Conchita had wandered out from the still noisy cantina to where Iron Eyes sat and picked up his plate as was her usual practice and something she had done countless times previously. The difference between her usual patrons and Iron Eyes was that unlike the local fishermen, this hideous creature had money and Conchita liked money. Especially the gringo variety.

The enterprising female could feel her heart pounding as she looked down upon the man with both his Navy Colts spread out before him on the table top. Sweat glistened on her exposed skin as she tried to draw his attention from the beach. She rested her hands on the table to either side of his plate and leaned forward. Her fully ripened breasts nearly fell from her white bodice as she vainly attempted to tempt him.

'I cannot wait to go to my rooms and rest upon my bed, Señor Iron Eyes,' she purred. 'But it is so lonely. You look as though you need a little rest. We could rest together.'

'I'll be just fine, ma'am,' he rasped. 'If you're tuckered then you should go and rest. Don't let me stop you.'

His response did not dampen her enthusiasm. Although she sensed that Iron Eyes was obviously dangerous, the thought of his golden eagles was too great. Conchita had already marked her twenty-fifth birthday and she knew that time was running out. If she could get enough money together, she could escape this village and head for somewhere more exciting.

There was no way Conchita could turn her back on such a prize, no matter what that prize looked like. She walked behind his wide shoulders and teased his long black hair.

'Is there anything else you require, Señor Iron

Eyes?' she asked with a hint of a woman who could ignore her own revulsion long enough to strip this horrendously scarred man of his money. Conchita bent over until her heavy bosom was close to his ear. 'Anything at all?'

Without looking up at the female, Iron Eyes gave a slight shake of his head.

'Nope. Just keep them friends of yours away from me,' he muttered in a low ominous growl. 'I ain't in the mood to be sociable.'

Daringly, Conchita remained bent over beside Iron Eyes, displaying her wares. The cotton fabric of her blouse was barely capable of restraining her breasts as she tried again to make him look at them. Yet the unblinking figure continued to stare straight ahead at the length of the beach.

'Maybe Conchita can soothe your tired body, Iron Eyes,' she suggested as the perfume from her cleavage filled his flared nostrils. 'I have a little room above the canteen. You could come with me there and I could be very nice to you.'

'I don't need no soothing, gal,' Iron Eyes grunted without moving a muscle. 'If you're tired you should go and take a rest.'

Conchita had not seen his brutalized features clearly since Iron Eyes had first arrived at the cantina. His long black hair hung over his face like a widow's veil. A mixture of vanity and bruised feelings swept through Conchita. She tried to remain calm but it was not easy, only the thought of his losing his money to another kept her by his shoulder.

'You don't want to make love to Conchita?' she whispered into his ear as her fingers toyed with strands of his hair. 'I do not charge much, Iron Eyes. I give you good time upstairs.'

'I'm fine right here,' the bounty hunter sighed.

'You do not understand, *señor*,' she continued. 'You look alone and I could keep you company if you like. It is not good for a fine man like you to be alone.'

'I ain't alone,' Iron Eyes grunted in a dismissive tone.

Conchita raised her eyebrows in surprise by his blunt statement. The floodgates of superstition engulfed her soul as her eyes vainly searched the cantina yard.

'Who is with you, *señor*? I see no one.'

'I see him,' Iron Eyes hissed. 'He's always with me.'

The attractive female clutched at her throat as her eyes darted to every shadow in fear. She swallowed hard.

'Who do you see, *señor*?'

Iron Eyes turned his head and looked into her large dark eyes. Strands of his unkempt mane fell away from his scarred features, revealing the atrocities that had maimed him forever. For the first time since his arrival, Conchita could see his mutilated features clearly. An uncontrollable whimper burst from her lovely lips.

'Death, Conchita,' he whispered. 'I see death. He's always with me riding on my shoulder. You can't see him, but he's here right enough. He's always here like a rattler waiting to sink his fangs in anyone he wants. One day it'll be my turn.'

His words made little sense to her. All she could do was stare at him in horror at the sight of his maimed face. She was unable to conceal her terror from him. Conchita diverted her eyes and gripped his plate in both her shaking hands.

'Are you afraid?' Conchita asked.

'There ain't no point in being fearful, gal.' Iron Eyes gave a shrug of his wide, bony shoulders. 'Death will get us all when he's ready. There's nothing we can do to stop him.'

The attractive young female straightened up. She was embarrassed by her outburst but still racked by terror. All thoughts of enticing this stranger up to her small room above the cantina were long gone.

'I'm so sorry, *señor*,' she stammered. 'I did not mean to yelp like a dog.'

Iron Eyes gave a nod of his head and focused on the crashing waves along the beach. He rested his hands on the table with his fingers spread out like the legs of a spider.

'Ain't no call for you to be upset, gal,' he drawled before lowering his chin until it touched his chest. 'I'm used to scaring critters.'

71

Tearfully the female scurried away and rushed back into the brightly illuminated cantina. The sound of its beaded curtain rang out like a toll of deathly bells. The bounty hunter glanced at the swaying beads for a brief heartbeat.

'Reckon I plumb scared her.' He grinned.

Iron Eyes returned his blistering attention to the beach and then pulled a long slim cigar from his deep trail coat pocket. He straightened it and placed it between his teeth. He recognized the look in her horrified face. It was one he had seen many times on many faces before.

His fingers located and struck the match across the wooden surface of the table and lifted it to the end of the long cigar. He sucked in the strong smoke and allowed it to fester in his lungs.

As it filtered back through his teeth, his bony fingers pulled the cork from the neck of the tequila bottle. Iron Eyes drew the cigar from his mouth and then lifted the bottle to his lips.

He took a long swallow and then placed the bottle down beside the five others and his guns. A dissatisfied grimace enveloped his face.

'That sure ain't whiskey,' he snorted as the fiery liquor burned a trail down to his guts. 'That tastes more like horse liniment. If they had more horses around here they wouldn't have to drink this stuff.'

With the cigar back between his teeth, the bounty hunter rose to his full height and scooped up the six bottles. He strode to where his mount was tethered and lifted one of the flaps of his saddle bags. He placed the bottles into the satchel cavity and then dropped the leather flap over them.

As his fingers went about securing the small buckle he heard another sound. It was totally different to the ruckus spilling out from the adobe cantina. Iron Eyes made his way back to where his guns lay on the table. He picked one up and dropped it into his bullet-filled pocket. Then he plucked the other Navy Colt off the wooden surface of the table and spun its chamber. Iron Eyes dropped his arm until the deadly six-shooter rested against his leg in readiness.

The familiar sound grew louder, like the steady rhythm of beating war drums. It echoed off the whitewashed structures which surrounded the gaunt bounty hunter. Even before he set eyes upon them, it became obvious what had drawn his attention.

It was the unmistakable noise of saddle horses as they approached the tiny fishing village. Iron Eyes listened to the pounding hoofs echoing all around him as he walked away from the colourful lanterns to the side of the adobe.

Iron Eyes lowered his head and glared through his bullet coloured eyes. The emaciated figure rested his shoulder against the corner of the cantina.

'I wonder who they are?' he hissed like a viper, ready to strike out at the horsemen if they got too close.

73

He stared out into the eerie moonlight. His eyes tightened in their sockets until they blazed. Both men were well-armed, he noted. These were not like anyone else he had encountered since travelling south of the border.

Whoever they were, they sure looked ready for trouble.

The pair of horsemen could be seen clearly in the bright moonlight as they steadily approached the coastal fishing village. They were unlike the villagers he had seen in and around the cantina.

'*Vaqueros,*' Iron Eyes spat and then returned the cigar to his mouth before filling his lungs with the smoke that fuelled him. 'That's the last thing I need. Stinking *vaqueros* paid to kill anyone who upsets their boss.'

Iron Eyes concentrated on the riders. He had had trouble with *vaqueros* a few times before and still bore the scars to prove it. The last thing the bounty hunter needed right now was locking antlers with their breed again.

Both riders wore wide-brimmed sombreros and sat astride tall handsome horses. Moonlight glanced across their weaponry and dazzled the eyes of their observer.

'They sure ain't peasants.' Iron Eyes snorted.

The horsemen drew closer.

As Iron Eyes watched them reduce the distance between themselves and the array of small adobes, his thumb pulled back on the hammer of the gun at his side until it locked into position. Then another idea struck the emaciated bounty hunter as he pondered who or what the riders might be. Could they be some of the blood-thirsty Mexican bandits who roamed freely across the border? If they were they might be here to put pay to the notorious hunter of wanted men.

News of Iron Eyes on the trail of the wanted outlaws had travelled fast, he thought. He wondered if they were the highly paid *vaqueros* who blindly obeyed their masters or the equally lethal bandits.

Neither theory sat well with Iron Eyes.

All he wanted to do was get his hands on Bodine and Walters and drag them back across the border. He had no stomach for wasting lead on fancy *vaqueros* or avenging bandits who had decided to kill the legendary bounty hunter.

Iron Eyes sucked the last smoke from his cigar and then spat it at the sand. His boot heel crushed the cigar as his eyes watched the horsemen getting closer with every beat of his heart.

His eyes burned through the limp strands of his hair as he watched the pair of horsemen slow their mounts to a canter. If he had to kill them, that was what he would do. Anyone who tried to kill Iron Eyes had already signed his own death sentence. Part of him was already dead. He knew that death already had one hand on his shoulder and one day would claim the rest of his emaciated carcass but until then he had no doubt that he would always get the better of those who challenged him.

For a man racked by the pain of countless ancient wounds, the thought of one day dying held no fear. For years Iron Eyes had hidden his pain from others with an abundant supply of strong cigars and the even stronger rot-gut whiskey. His senses were dulled to everything apart from the instinct to kill.

Iron Eyes grunted with amusement as the riders entered the small village and headed straight at him.

He eased his tall frame away from the wall and walked from the shadows and stood squarely in the middle of the sandy trail road and awaited them.

The horsemen rode through the eerie moonlight toward him.

Not a muscle in his body moved.

'Keep on coming, boys,' he snarled as his finger stroked the trigger of his weapon. 'If you're looking for a fight, you came to the right place.'

NINE

Pablo Fernandez had become aware that his prized stallion was nervous long before his eyes caught sight of the eerie figure that stood defiantly in the middle of the sandy street. The son of the noble Don Jose watched as Iron Eyes waited fifty yards from where he and his obedient *vaquero* sat astride their lathered up mounts.

Pablo pulled back on his reins and stopped his tall horse abruptly. His hireling eased back on his own leathers and stared through the eerie light at the gruesome sight that faced them.

'I think we have located our prey, Luis,' Pablo said as he steadied his nervous mount.

'What kind of devil is that, Pablo?' the *vaquero* asked as he watched the death defying bounty hunter.

'I have only heard stories about him, Luis,' Pablo admitted as he pulled an ornate silver cigar case from his breast pocket and opened it. 'The stories do not do Iron Eyes justice.'

Both men watched the haunting figure turn sideways so that his gaunt frame made an even narrower target. Pablo pulled a cigar from the case and tapped it on the silver lid. His eyes never left the horrific sight before them as he placed the long smoke between his lips and slid the case back into his pocket.

'I do not think this is going to be as easy as I thought, Luis,' he said. 'He does not look in the mood to either talk or listen, *amigo*.'

'So that is Iron Eyes?' Luis mumbled as he gripped his reins firmly in his gloved hands. 'He looks like no man I have ever set eyes upon before, *amigo*.'

There was no arguing with that fact. Iron Eyes resembled a corpse that had just clawed its way out of a grave more than he did a living man. But the bounty hunter was real enough and he was standing directly before them. Few creatures of any kind could chill the blood of those who gazed upon his deathly appearance but Iron Eyes had mastered that long ago.

Without taking his eyes off the devilish bounty hunter for even a heartbeat, Pablo struck a match, cupped its flame and raised it to the cigar between his lips. He sucked the flame into the cigar and brooded upon the man that Don Jose had sent them to bring back to the hacienda. Then he exhaled.

Smoke billowed from his mouth and extinguished the match.

'You are right, old friend,' he agreed. 'He is nothing like other men. Maybe some of those stories about him are true. Maybe he is dead like they say.'

The shocked *vaquero* glanced at Pablo.

'Dead?' he repeated. 'You say that we are risking our necks against a dead man? You might not have thought about this but facing a dead man is loco. We cannot kill something that no longer lives but he could kill us.'

'That is just the legend, *amigo*,' Pablo replied through a cloud of smoke. 'The Indians say he is a living ghost. A man who must be feared because he cannot die like all other creatures. Such things are fairy tales.'

'He looks dead, though,' Luis gulped.

'I agree.' Pablo frowned. 'He certainly looks dead.'

Sweat trailed down from the dust-laden sombrero of the hired gunman as he listened to the unsettling words. He looked at the haunting figure ahead of them and then returned his eyes to his smoking companion.

'That is impossible, Pablo,' Luis nervously ventured as his eyes strained to see even a hint of humanity in the deathly form of Iron Eyes. 'Men are either dead or they are alive. They cannot be both, can they?'

Before Fernandez could answer, he noticed that the infamous bounty hunter was raising his free hand. He watched as long thin fingers pushed the limp strands of dark hair from his face.

The sight of his maimed features caught the unforgiving moonlight as Iron Eyes stared across the distance at them. The spawn of Satan was watching them.

'Santa Maria,' Luis gasped.

The cigar hung from Pablo's trembling lips for a few moments before he plucked it from his mouth and glanced at his terrified companion.

'I think it is time for us to announce ourselves to Iron Eyes, *amigo*,' he stammered before placing his hand on the crest of his saddle horn and slowly dismounting.

'I think this man will not like what you have to say, Pablo.' Luis sighed as he threw his leg over his cantle and dropped to the ground. He gripped the reins of his skittish mount and moved closer to the younger man. 'He looks very angry now and he does not even know that we have already taken his woman. I think the news will upset him.'

Thoughtfully, Fernandez gripped the bridle of his nervous mount. He wondered if the infamous gringo might start shooting before he had time to explain the facts.

'You might be correct, *amigo*.' Pablo straightened up and tossed his reins to his hireling. 'Guard the horses. I think that they might turn and run away from here if the shooting starts.'

Luis took the reins and sucked in his lower lip. 'They will not be alone if they run away, Pablo.'

Fernandez defied his own fear and began to walk slowly toward the brooding bounty hunter. Every step was watched by the unblinking eyes of Iron Eyes.

As the handsome Mexican approached, Pablo felt his fear growing inside him. To walk toward Iron Eyes was like walking toward your own grave. He stared at the bounty hunter's blazing eyes as they burned into him. Even the moonlight could not dampen their fury.

Pablo stopped.

Both men were now only twenty feet apart. Dust floated around the spurs of the Mexican as he tried to collect his thoughts. Iron Eyes was coiled and ready to strike and the younger man knew it. Then Fernandez made a mistake. He innocently raised his hand to his jacket pocket to retrieve a letter his father had written.

The move was too sudden and too fast.

Thinking that he was facing an arrogant unknown bandit, the gaunt figure reacted in the only fashion he knew.

Like quicksilver, Iron Eyes swung on his heels and raised the Navy Colt. His bony finger pulled back on his weapons trigger.

A flash of blinding flame exploded from the seven

inch long barrel and tore through the moonlight. At the same moment a deafening sound rocked the fishing village like a thunderclap.

The narrowed eyes of the bounty hunter waited for the gun smoke to disperse as his bony thumb pulled back his gun hammer until it locked into position once more.

TEN

Believing that Fernandez was attempting to draw down on him, Iron Eyes had raised and blasted his gun in the time it normally takes for a normal person to spit. But the only spitting came from the long barrel of the Navy Colt. A twisting, blinding flash had erupted from the gun in the skeletal hand and sent lead at the young Mexican.

Somehow the bullet had not hit Pablo as it hit the wide brim of the Mexican's sombrero.

The drawstring under Pablo's chin had snapped as his sombrero was ripped from his head by the sudden and violent impact of the shot. Pablo stood staring at the deadly bounty hunter as a trickle of blood trailed down his face from his well-oiled hair. He was shaking as the smoke cleared before his unblinking eyes.

He steadied himself and looked across at the uncanny figure before him. Smoke trailed from the

83

barrel of the gun in Iron Eyes's claw-like hand. Then he noticed that the gun was trained at his chest.

'Are you OK?' Luis called out from behind him as the *vaquero* fought to keep both their terrified horses under control.

Slowly Pablo raised a hand and signalled to his muscular friend. 'Do not do anything, Luis. Señor Iron Eyes is too good a shot for the likes of us.'

Iron Eyes stared with gritted teeth at the startled Mexican. 'Who are you varmints?'

Pablo Fernandez licked his dry lips. 'We are just messengers, *señor.*'

The bounty hunter kept the six-shooter aimed at the young Mexican and forced a twisted smile. He remained totally still.

'You did not kill me,' Pablo said fearfully as he looked at the Navy Colt. 'But I think that you still might.'

Iron Eyes rose to his full height but kept the smoking weapon trained on Fernandez. The mutilated face looked out from behind the veil of hair.

'Yes, I still might kill you,' he drawled. 'If I figure you need killing then I'll oblige. Do you need killing, sonny? Are you wanted with a price on your head? Who the hell are you?'

'My name is Pablo Fernandez, *señor,*' the younger man managed to say as he made sure his gun hand remained well away from his holstered pistol. His fingers found the graze across his scalp. He stared at the blood on his fingertips and gulped.

Iron Eyes did not move a muscle as his mind raced. He stared intently at Fernandez as he recalled hearing the name before. He then marched up to the bleeding Mexican and pointed his gun at him.

'I've heard your name before, ain't I?' he rasped as his finger stroked the trigger of his Navy Colt. 'Remind me where I've heard your name before, Pablo boy.'

Fernandez sucked in air and bit his lower lip.

'My father is Don Jose Fernandez,' he answered.

Iron Eyes chewed on the name. 'Didn't that varmint send a couple of his *vaqueros* across the border a while back?'

'*Sí, señor.*' Pablo nodded. 'We need to hire your services on a vital matter.'

'I ain't no hired gun, boy.' Iron Eyes released his gun hammer and pushed the still smoking barrel behind his buckle into his belt. 'I'm a bounty hunter. I don't hire out to folks who want to avenge their grievances.'

'You explained this to my father's men,' Pablo reminded the deadly man. 'You explained this very brutally.'

'I don't like *vaqueros*,' the bounty hunter snarled. 'They was lucky I didn't kill them.'

'This is most urgent, *señor*,' Pablo pressed. 'A matter of life and death. You must listen.'

'I don't hire out to fancy dudes like you, sonny.' Iron Eyes turned and started back to the cantina when the words that left Pablo's mouth stopped him in his tracks.

'My father has detained Squirrel Sally, Iron Eyes,' Pablo said. 'He has your woman.'

Like a volcano ready to erupt into unimaginable fury, the tall bounty hunter looked over his shoulder at the bleeding Mexican. He slowly turned and glared at Pablo.

'Your pappy has done what?' he growled.

'He has your woman, *señor*. He said that you would not listen to his request so he has become a little more aggressive.'

Iron Eyes lowered his head but kept his burning eyes on the terrified young man. He clenched his fists and gritted his teeth.

'He's got Squirrel?' the bounty hunter hissed with venomous anger. 'My Squirrel?'

Pablo nodded. '*Sí, señor*. He will kill her if you do not help him. My father is desperate and men who are desperate become very dangerous.'

'I'm dangerous, sonny.' Iron Eyes snorted. 'Far more dangerous than your pappy imagines. If he harms one hair on that gal's head, I'll kill him and everyone he has ever cherished.'

Pablo backed away from the raging bounty hunter. He kept the palms of his hands raised and facing the notorious Iron Eyes. With each backward step he watched as Iron Eyes closed the distance between them.

'Please, *señor*,' Pablo pleaded. 'We are just the messengers. All my father wants is that you come and hear why he wants to hire you. I am sure he will pay you for your time.'

Iron Eyes stopped.

'Why the hell does he want me to help him?' he shouted. 'What kinda dirty job does your pappy think that only I can do? I don't get it, boy. This country is full of scum-suckers who'll hire out and do anything for a price. How come he wants me?'

Pablo lowered his head. 'Because you are Iron Eyes, *señor*. Only you are brave enough to do what has to be done.'

Iron Eyes leapt at the Mexican. He grabbed Fernandez by the lapels and pulled him to him. Every fibre of his being wanted to kill both of the men but the bounty hunter knew that to do so was not going to free the perky Squirrel Sally.

'I ain't gonna kill you just yet, boy,' he snarled into the face of the younger man before releasing his grip and pushing him toward the horses. 'But if any of your clan harms that gal, you'll all be dead. Savvy?'

Iron Eyes turned away from both the horsemen and started to stride toward the cantina. Pablo rubbed his neck and then called out at the wide back of the bounty hunter.

'Where are you going, *Señor* Iron Eyes?'

87

'To get my horse,' Iron Eyes growled without turning as he rounded the corner of the well-illuminated building. 'Then you're gonna take me to meet your pappy.'

Pablo nodded and pulled the letter from his pocket. 'You must read my father's note.'

A few moments after the scrawny figure had vanished behind the whitewashed walls of the still rowdy cantina, Iron Eyes emerged into the moonlight. He jabbed his spurs into the flanks of the magnificent stallion and rode to the men.

He stopped the palomino beside the men and watched as Fernandez mounted his horse. Pablo reached out with the crumpled letter in his shaking hand but Iron Eyes did not accept it.

'Your pappy can speak to me face to face, Fernandez,' he hissed. 'Besides, I only read Wanted posters.'

The three horsemen thundered into the moonlight.

ELEVEN

Squirrel Sally could not understand what was going on. She had been offered fresh clothing, a bath and fed on the finest food. Don Jose had ushered her into a first floor room as he would have done to a valued guest. The feisty female could not understand what was happening but the rifle toting *vaquero* positioned outside her room made it clear that she was not a guest.

She was a prisoner.

No amount of fancy trimmings could alter that fact. She was being held in the hacienda against her will and no matter how charming everyone was to her, Sally felt sure that she would be shot if she dared to try and escape. She knew this was a trap to capture her beloved Iron Eyes and that she was the bait.

After hours of fretting, weariness finally overtook her best efforts to remain awake. She sank into the soft mattress and slept like she had never slept before. The perfumed bath water had relaxed her tiny body as its soothing scent filled her trail-tired mind.

A soothing carpet of tranquil dreams displaced the concerns that had dogged her since she had been dragged cursing into the magnificent edifice. Yet as Sally slept, the rest of the fortified hacienda awaited the arrival of the fearsome Iron Eyes.

Downstairs, beneath the vaulted ceiling of the main room, the ruler of this land stood beside his fireplace with one foot on the grate and watched the flames as they twisted up the chimney. The large logs crackled as they were devoured, but Don Jose heard nothing apart from what was going on in his court-yard.

The sound of his small army as they moved around the courtyard echoed off the high walls but did nothing to ease his trepidation. The nobleman had done the unthinkable and sent for the one man who was feared more than the Devil himself.

Don Jose inhaled the final dregs of his cigar and then tossed it on to the logs. As the strong smoke slowly escaped from beneath his well-trimmed cigar, he turned and stared at the open doors.

The nobleman had done many things in his long life that he regretted, but nothing to equal this. He had resorted to kidnapping an innocent female in order to lure one of the most dangerous men on both sides of the border to him. He needed the help of the one man he knew capable of helping him, but he was still filled with regret. There was no knowing what Iron Eyes might do when he eventually arrived.

All he could do was await the inevitable.

Fernandez walked across the vast room toward the open doors. The sound of his steps echoed off the floor tiles as he reached the torch lit yard.

His eyes glanced around its expanse. Squirrel Sally's stagecoach was parked close to the covered stable where her team of six horses were being watered and grained. He then studied the riflemen on the parapet that surrounded his home.

The sound of approaching horses drew his attention to the gates. Fernandez looked up to the sentry on its high walkway.

'Are they coming?' he shouted.

The *vaquero* nodded and turned to look down on his master.

'*Sí*, Don Jose,' he said, clutching his rifle across his chest. 'I can make out Pablo and Luis. There is another rider with them. He is atop a palomino.'

Fernandez nodded and sighed.

He had heard about the palomino stallion the infamous bounty hunter had been riding for the last few years. His son had found Iron Eyes and was bringing him to him just as instructed. No matter how hard he tried, though, Don Jose could not shake off the feeling that he was inviting a fox into his hen house.

Had he bitten off more than he could chew? Soon he would discover the answer.

A bead of sweat defied the cool evening temperature and rolled down the face of the elegant Fernandez. He sensed that soon he would learn how much the notorious bounty hunter cared for the small female.

Most men would comply with the overwhelming odds that were stacked against them. Most would realize that it was futile to try and resist the many guns that guarded Don Jose and his prisoner. They would do as they were told for fear of what might happen if they did not.

But Iron Eyes was not like other men.

He never did what you expected him to do. For all the nobleman knew, Iron Eyes would start shooting as soon as he entered the courtyard. Don Jose moved to the edge of the wooden boardwalk that surrounded the hacienda and he placed his trembling hand on the ivory grip of his holstered pistol. Yet he knew that if the stories about the deadly bounty hunter were only half true, he would never be able to draw his gun before Iron Eyes had dispatched him.

What had seemed like a good plan was now becoming more and more worrying. Iron Eyes had already unleashed his fury on the *vaqueros* Don Jose had sent north of the border in a vain bid to hire his services. He began to doubt that kidnapping the fiery female to lure him to his hacienda would mellow the notorious bounty hunter into submission.

In fact, it could have the totally opposite effect. Iron Eyes might not be in any mood to either listen or help the nobleman, having had his woman snatched in the dark.

Don Jose felt his heart pounding inside his frilly shirt.

Had he opened Pandora's Box? Were they bringing a nest of vipers into the heart of his home? Sweat trailed down his moonlit profile as he stared fearfully at the open gates and the armed sentries upon its parapets.

Don Jose knew that many men build walls to keep their enemies out when in fact those same walls can also keep their worst nightmares trapped within.

'Don Jose,' one of the sentries shouted out as he pointed his gleaming rifle at the approaching trio of horsemen. 'They are nearly here.'

Fernandez gave a nod as his eyes darted around the interior of the torch-lit courtyard. The blood-soaked legend of the infamous bounty hunter flashed through his mind. He prayed that it was an exaggeration but feared that it was more likely a watered down version of the truth.

Don Jose swallowed hard but his throat was as dry as the surrounding desert. It was now too late to do anything but pray that he might be able to explain his reasons for bringing both Squirrel Sally and Iron

Eyes to his home before the bounty hunter started to unleash his fury.

The sound of the three horses grew louder. Their hoof beats echoed off the whitewashed walls all around the fortified hacienda.

Then he saw them enter the courtyard.

Fernandez could not take his unblinking eyes off the horseman riding behind his son and the *vaquero*. He took a faltering step forward and stared at the rider. The blazing torches spilled their crimson light on to the unearthly entity.

A terror gripped the nobleman.

Don Jose had never been so frightened before by the horrific sight that approached him. The long limp hair flapped on the wide shoulders of Iron Eyes as his skeletal face stared with unblinking eyes down at him.

Fernandez was looking straight into the face of death as the high-shouldered palomino stallion cantered toward him. His heart was fit to burst as every one of the gruesome stories he had heard concerning the deadly hunter of men filled his mind. He wanted to run but his feet were glued to the spot. All he could do was watch the devilish horseman as he bore down on him.

His wide open eyes watched in horror as the scarlet torchlight bathed Iron Eyes in its fiery hue. What sort of creature had he invited into the inner sanctum of his home?

94

Was this Satan? Fernandez would soon discover the answer.

TWELVE

The spires of solid rock loomed up from the desert floor like the fingers of some unearthly monster vainly trying to rip the large moon out of the sky. The moonlight cast its uninterrupted illumination down from the cloudless heavens as though the gods themselves wanted to find the elusive Running Wolf and his followers.

Black shadows in total contrast to the light spread out from the impressive mesas and ridges of ancient stone. In every shadow it was said a dozen or more eyes watched the braver creatures who rode through the eerie light.

Yet there were eyes in many of the shadows that tapered away from the massive monoliths. They were the eyes of the rebel Apaches who guarded the solitary trail path that led through a splintered boulder and into a place few even knew existed.

An arch of stone rose from one side of the trail to

the other. It was said that to ride beneath the archway was to invoke the wrath of the gods but as it was the only way down into the hidden valley, few heeded the ominous warnings preached by generations of tribal medicine men.

This was how the place had first gotten its name.

Devil's Cradle was a fertile valley fed by crystal clear water that made its way down from the imposing mesas in defiance of the heat which had slowly burned everything beyond its granite walls and turned them to ash.

Only the keenest of eyes would have even realized that there was such a fertile land set in the otherwise arid desolation but Running Wolf had. After fleeing the retribution of the homesteaders and army north of the unmarked border, he had headed down to the vast, sun-baked desert toward Costa Angelo. His keen instincts soon noticed the tell-tale signs around the lush valley.

Just like the formidable Iron Eyes, Running Wolf had spent his life hunting all types of game in a multitude of terrains and could read the land as easily as some read the printed word. After nearly a year of moving his dwindling band of followers from one encampment to another, he noticed the strange rocky spires that towered above everything else within the parched region.

It had not taken the ruthless Apache long to find Devil's Cradle. Running Wolf had used the secluded

97

gulch as a base for his increasingly small army of Apache rebels. They constructed more permanent dwellings as time rolled on, but Running Wolf and his score of lethal killers still raided homesteads and attacked forts when it suited them. There seemed to be no logical explanation in their attacks but to men who had seen their way of life destroyed by the ceaseless invasion of intruders, there did not have to be a reason.

Geronimo and Sitting Bull had each proclaimed at different times that they would kill all those who defiled their land and send all of their enemies back to where they had come from. It eventually dawned on them that there were simply too many to either kill or send retreating.

They had fought valiant fights but knew it was impossible to stem the flow of this wound. Geronimo and Sitting Bull had been wise enough to know that although they had won many battles they had lost the war.

Running Wolf had not been as wise as his cousins.

Even knowing that his days were numbered he had continued to make brutal raids on both sides of the border for precious livestock and food provisions, but it was his taking of female prisoners of any age, which had caused the most revulsion.

Many of the females' relatives had vainly tried to find their loved ones but none had ever been successful in their quest. Death had struck down all those who had attempted to enter the legendary Devil's Cradle with brutal and merciless retribution.

The Devil's Cradle had been a safe haven nobody could either locate or penetrate to recover the females who had been trapped within. But was it?

Was that about to change with the arrival of Iron Eyes in the region? Would even the most lethal of bounty hunters dare to challenge the merciless Running Wolf and the even more formidable Devil's Cradle?

Death was said to await all those who dared approach the infamous Devil's Cradle and try to enter its uncharted terrain, but there were a few who did not fear death.

Iron Eyes was one of them.

THIRTEEN

The sandy beaches that fringed Costa Angelo were still shrouded in the cloak of darkness as storm clouds gently moved across the heavens and blocked the bright moon. The row boat that Walters and Bodine had used to make their escape was finally returning to the shore, but few noticed its return.

Waves broke in sickening succession along the countless miles of sand. They started to resemble bronco-busters as they crashed into the shore. Then the row boat rode one of the shoulder high rollers and came down heavily into the wet sand.

The sound of its wooden skeleton being broken was lost in the deafening noise of the continuous incoming tide. Planks of wood were ripped from the body of the small fishing boat and sent in various directions as it was pounded by the brutal power that only oceans can muster.

As the boat twisted and turned, a few of the local

fishermen raced down from the small group of adobes and attempted to haul what was left of it ashore.

It was a futile effort.

As the hands of the villagers dragged the water-logged vessel up on to the dry sand, they wondered how one of their best fishing boats could have ended up like this.

The mast had gone and whoever had been within the boat had also suffered the same fate. As the men rested and looked into the bowels of the row boat, a few more of the small village's inhabitants joined them from the cantina.

The buxom Conchita looked at the wreckage and then began to recall that which Iron Eyes had uttered to her earlier.

'He said that he was waiting for a boat to return to the shore,' she said as one of the fishermen stared at her.

'Who did?' he asked.

'Iron Eyes. He was expecting a boat and here it is,' Conchita said the name and then felt a cold chill trace her spine. She shivered and pulled her shawl up over her shoulders. 'I do not understand.'

A silver-haired man placed his hand on her shoulder. 'Whoever stole this fishing boat has paid the price for his crime, Conchita. The sea has taken them.'

Conchita turned and began walking back to the

101

cantina. As she reached the ridge she stopped.

She looked at one of the other fishermen. 'Did you see the strange gringo drinking in the yard of the cantina?'

The man shook his head.

'I did not see anyone, my little one,' he answered and continued up the dune to the array of coloured lanterns. 'Maybe you dreamed of him.'

Conchita shivered. 'Iron Eyes does not inhabit dreams. He is the thing nightmares are made of.'

FOURTEEN

Not even the darkest of shadows could have hidden the fear and trepidation that was carved into the faces of both Pablo and Luis as they led the gaunt bounty hunter toward Don Jose. By the expressions on their faces it was obvious that neither of them were in control of the stranger they had just escorted into the spacious yard. His Navy Colts could be seen poking out from behind his belt buckle. Iron Eyes was ready to draw and start killing at any moment.

Like a man watching the approach of his own death, Don Jose Fernandez simply stared at the gruesome figure riding a few paces behind his son and the *vaquero*. As the three horsemen passed beneath the flaming torches and continued on toward him, his fear grew.

Pablo drew rein as his mount reached the spot where his father stood. He gave a nod to the older man but Don Jose did not return the greeting.

Fernandez could not take his eyes off the hideous features of the rider astride the palomino. Never in all of his days had he ever imagined anything that resembled Iron Eyes. This was the remnants of a man who somehow refused to die. His brutalized features glanced around his surroundings yet it was impossible to tell what was going through his mind.

The mixture of moonlight and torchlight gave the bounty hunter the look of something that was dead but too angry to acknowledge the fact.

The older man stepped back as Iron Eyes steered the stallion toward him. Iron Eyes dragged his long leathers up to his chest and stopped the snorting palomino. He then hung over the creamy mane of the powerful animal and glared down at Don Jose.

'Are you the varmint that stole Squirrel?' he snorted.

'*Sí, señor.*' Don Jose knew that every rifle was trained on the bounty hunter but it did not make him feel any safer. His face twitched as he watched Iron Eyes loop his leg over his saddle cantle and slowly dismount.

Iron Eyes held the bridle firmly in his hand and studied the far smaller man bathed in the lantern light which flowed from the open doorway behind him.

'Answer me this,' Iron Eyes growled. 'Why did you kidnap my Squirrel?'

Without opening his mouth, Don Jose shrugged.

Iron Eyes straightened up to his full height. His eyes darted around the riflemen atop the parapets and then returned to Don Jose.

'You'd better not have hurt her,' he warned.

'We have not harmed her, *señor*,' Don Jose finally managed to say. 'We only brought her here in order to get an audience with you. I am desperate to talk with you.'

Iron Eyes tossed his reins into the hands of Luis and marched to the side of Fernandez. 'Feed and water my horse.'

The *vaquero* rode toward the stables with the palomino in tow and Pablo dismounted. The younger Fernandez followed his father and the tall bounty hunter into the well-lit house.

'I am grateful that you decided to come here to help me, *señor*,' Don Jose said as he walked toward a table filled with an array of decanters, each filled with a different coloured liquor.

Iron Eyes trailed him to the decanters and lifted the one with the darkest contents. He pulled its stopper and allowed its familiar aroma to fill his flared nostrils.

'I didn't come here to help you, Fernandez,' he muttered before moving to a well-padded chair with the glass decanter in his hand. He sat down and watched the father and son as they anxiously trailed him. 'I come here to get Squirrel.'

Don Jose sat opposite his fearsome guest and

watched as the bounty hunter drank from the decanter.

'Did you not read my letter, *señor*?' he asked. 'I have detailed everything in it concerning the reasons for our kidnapping your woman.'

'I didn't read it,' the bounty hunter drawled.

'But you still came to rescue your woman,' Don Jose said.

Iron Eyes lowered the decanter. 'Squirrel ain't my woman, Fernandez. She's a thorn in my side, but she ain't my woman.'

Pablo looked surprised. 'But she said she was.'

'Squirrel sure thinks she is.' Iron Eyes accepted a cigar and then scratched his thumbnail across a match and sucked in its smoke. 'It's plumb pitiful, but for some reason she just won't quit.'

'But you risked your life coming here to rescue her.' Don Jose looked baffled. 'If she isn't your woman why would you do this, *señor*?'

Ignoring the question, Iron Eyes placed the decanter on the floor beside his boot and then inhaled more smoke into his emaciated body. He shrugged and stared straight at Don Jose.

'Tell me why you lured me here?' he scowled. 'I was waiting for two valuable outlaws to show themselves back at a tiny fishing village when I got diverted.'

'The outlaws are in our pay, *señor*,' Pablo admitted. 'We paid them to lead you to Costa Angelo.'

106

Iron Eyes narrowed his eyes. 'Walters and Bodine led me here?'

Pablo nodded nervously.

'My young daughter has been kidnapped by Apaches, *señor*,' Don Jose revealed bluntly. 'She was taken as she was being escorted here.'

'Just like you done to little Squirrel.' Iron Eyes showed no interest as he tapped ash on to the tiled floor. 'Why should I get involved?'

The elder Fernandez lowered his head and started to sob. His son placed a comforting hand on his father's shoulder and looked straight at the bounty hunter.

'My little sister is only six years of age, *Señor* Iron Eyes,' Pablo said sadly. 'She was taken by Running Wolf and his rebels.'

Suddenly Iron Eyes looked interested. He leaned forward and stared at the elderly man. To the bounty hunter it seemed strange that anyone of Don Jose's advancing years should have a daughter so young.

'Running Wolf the Apache rebel?' Iron Eyes repeated the warrior's name as his mind began to recall that there was a bounty on the Indian's head. A very big bounty as he recalled. 'He's worth more than both them outlaws combined.'

Don Jose nodded as his hands automatically joined together as if in silent prayer.

'Your government has been hunting Running Wolf for over a decade, *señor*,' he said. 'I believe that he has been raiding ranches across the border and making it very hard for settlers and your army.'

The notion of a defenceless six-year-old being at the mercy of the infamous Running Wolf did not sit well with Iron Eyes. He stood and moved to the fire and rested a thoughtful hand upon its mantle.

'Running Wolf is a mighty valuable catch,' he muttered as his teeth gripped the cigar as smoke drifted into his scarred face. 'The US Army will pay handsomely if I could bring that critter to them. They've bin chasing him longer than they've bin hunting Geronimo.'

'He is wanted dead or alive, *señor*,' Pablo said.

Iron Eyes nodded. 'That means dead in my book, sonny,' he drawled through cigar smoke. 'I don't take prisoners. It don't pay in my profession.'

Don Jose stood and walked to the side of the tall ghostly figure. He rested a hand on the blood-stained trail coat and spoke quietly.

'I will pay you to bring my daughter back, Iron Eyes,' he said softly. 'I know it is doubtful that she still lives but I will pay you anyway.'

'She's still alive, Fernandez,' Iron Eyes said bluntly. 'She's young and a female. Running Wolf and his kind like them that way.'

A horrified expression filled the face of the nobleman as he gasped. 'Santa Maria. You mean. . . .'

'Yep.' Iron Eyes nodded.

Pablo clenched both his fists. 'We must get her

away from them, Señor Iron Eyes. There is not a moment to lose.'

'It might already be too late,' the bounty hunter hissed as he chewed on the cigar between his teeth. 'Mind you, she is real young. Maybe too young even for them but time moves fast and the longer she's with them, the more likely it is that they'll do their worst.'

'You must help us rescue her,' Fernandez pleaded.

Iron Eyes glanced over his shoulder at the face of the well-groomed man. He had seen that desperate look before.

'How much are you willing to pay for me to help rescue your little girl, Don Jose?' he asked curiously.

'One hundred golden eagles,' Fernandez replied. 'I have had them brought straight from the mint in San Francisco. They are yours, whatever your decision.'

The face of the bounty hunter looked surprised.

'You're willing to give me a hundred gold eagles whatever I choose to do?'

The older man looked at the flames as they leapt up the chimney. He was a broken soul who had resigned himself to the inevitable.

'*Sí, señor*,' Fernandez said. 'You can have it and Squirrel Sally too. All I want is my daughter. I have lost ten *vaqueros* trying to rescue her and those who are left are as broken as I am.'

Iron Eyes sucked in more smoke as he thought

109

about the offer. He began to nod and then swung on his heels and paced back to where he left his drink. He bent down and scooped up the decanter. Both the Fernandezes watched as the haunting figure finished off the contents of the glass vessel. Neither dared utter a word as the bounty hunter checked his firearms and placed them in his deep trail coat pockets.

Iron Eyes looked at both men in turn.

'You got any images of the little girl?' he asked.

A smile etched the face of Don Jose. He rushed to a circular table set near a bookcase and picked up a silver frame. For a moment he hesitated as his elderly eyes looked at the photographic likeness protected by glass. Then he inhaled deeply and walked to where the painfully lean bounty hunter stood.

His shaking hand gave the framed picture to the grim-faced Iron Eyes. Don Jose watched as the bounty hunter removed the picture from its frame and stared at it under the light of a chandelier suspended from the ceiling. There was no visible expression on the face of the bounty hunter as his eyes studied the image in his hands.

'That is my Maria,' Fernandez said proudly. 'She is the image of her late mother. I do not have any more images of Maria. Please take care of it.'

Iron Eyes responded to the sadness in Fernandez's faltering voice. His bullet coloured eyes darted at the face of the elderly man for a moment and then returned to the picture in his bony hands.

'I don't need it, Fernandez,' he said coldly. 'I got her looks branded into my mind. I'll recognize her if our paths cross.'

'Thank you, *señor*,' Don Jose gushed as he held the photograph to his chest.

'You do understand that your Maria might have bin taken as a bride, don't you, Don Jose?' Iron Eyes whispered. 'Apaches don't have rules on such things like most folks.'

Don Jose sighed heavily.

'I just want her back,' he said. 'I just want her back.'

Iron Eyes looked at Pablo. He raised a finger and pointed at the younger man.

'Can you take me to where the coach was attacked, sonny?' he asked as he watched Don Jose carefully putting the picture back into its frame. 'I need to start my hunt from the exact spot the coach came to a rest.'

Pablo stepped toward the heavily scarred figure that was standing in the centre of the room. He tilted his head and stared at Iron Eyes.

'But it has been too long since Maria was taken for there to be any tracks remaining, *señor*,' he said. 'There is no way that you could track Running Wolf from there.'

Iron Eyes gave a twisted grin.

'I know that, boy,' he muttered. 'But I'll get me a

111

sense of where his camp is. A cougar never travels far from his lair and Running Wolf is just a two-legged big cat. I'll figure out where he's holed up when I see the place he attacked the caravan.'

'You make it sound simple, *señor*,' Don Jose said as he placed the silver framed picture back on the table and turned to look at the formidable bounty hunter.

'It is simple, Don Jose.' Iron Eyes placed the cigar back between his teeth and gripped it. 'Even the most ruthless of killers return to their lair. That's how a hunter can get them in his gun sights and kill them. You just gotta be able to figure out where they rest their bones at night.'

Pablo edged closer to the bounty hunter. 'But Running Wolf and his followers are nomads, Señor Iron Eyes. They are continually moving their camp. By now they could be hundreds of miles from here.'

Iron Eyes looked through the smoke which drifted up from his cigar. His twisted smile grew even wider.

'I hope he has moved camp, sonny,' he drawled. 'That'll leave a fresh trail to follow.'

'I have a room ready for you, *señor*,' Don Jose announced as he moved between the two younger men. 'It is the same room that your woman occupies. You can rest until the sun rises once more.'

Iron Eyes pulled the cigar from his lips and shook his head until his mane of long black hair covered his mutilated features.

'I don't need no room to rest, Fernandez,' he

growled. 'I'm heading out now to the spot where your coach was attacked and little Maria was taken from. There ain't no time to go visiting Squirrel.'

Don Jose looked stunned. 'You do not wish to see if we have treated your woman kindly, *señor*?'

Iron Eyes paced around the room. The spurs on his boots rang out as he thoughtfully circled the two men.

'Squirrel can look after herself,' he muttered. 'Besides, she ain't my woman. She's just a burr under my saddle. That gal troubles me something awful.'

'I shall get fresh horses ready, Señor Iron Eyes,' Pablo said, before marching across the tiled floor and walking out into the courtyard.

Don Jose moved in front of the tall shadowy figure and looked up at the well-hidden face. The glowing tip of the cigar grew brighter with every breath the bounty hunter took.

'You are an honourable man, *señor*,' he said. 'You had the choice of taking the money without doing anything but you have chosen to risk your life and try to rescue my daughter. I shall get the one hundred golden eagles for you now.'

As the Mexican went to move away from Iron Eyes, a thin hand gripped Don Jose's shoulder and stopped him. The older man glanced back at the unlikely hero.

'What, my boy?' he enquired. 'Why do you stop me getting your money?'

Iron Eyes shook his hair off his face and straightened up to his full height. He stared at the arched ceiling without looking into the eyes of the noble Don Jose.

'One hundred gold coins are too heavy for me to go hunting with, old man,' he said as he swung on his heels and started to follow the path Pablo had taken out into the moonlight. 'They'd slow me down. You keep them until I get back.'

'But what if fate is against you, *señor*?' Fernandez asked. 'What if you suffer the same fate which befell my *vaqueros* and do not return?'

'Then give the money to Squirrel,' Iron Eyes muttered.

Don Jose Fernandez watched as the dishevelled man approached the wide open doors. He could not understand the man who no longer resembled other men but something deep inside him felt confident that he had made the right choice in sending for the legendary Iron Eyes.

The bounty hunter paused.

'What is wrong, *señor*?' Don Jose asked.

Iron Eyes looked around the magnificent interior of the hacienda and then looked at the elegant Fernandez. He did not speak as his teeth gripped the smouldering cigar. He touched his brow and then walked out into the courtyard. Even though he now knew that probably the most valuable creature he had ever tracked was out there somewhere amid the

114

arid terrain and inhospitable mesas, there was another reason for the ravaged bounty hunter to set out on this suicidal mission.

Her name was Maria Fernandez. She was six years old and her image was branded into his memory where it would remain until he found her.

Few things ever put a flame to his fuse but the monochrome face on the small picture in its silver frame had done so. She was the helpless victim who probably had no notion of what was happening to her.

Iron Eyes stepped down on to the sand and watched as Pablo emerged from the stable with two long-legged horses in tow. The bounty hunter watched silently as the handsome young man walked ahead of the thoroughbreds toward him. His narrowed eyes noted that one of the animals was wearing his palomino stallion's livery.

'How far is it to where Running Wolf attacked the coach, Pablo?' Iron Eyes asked as he fumbled in his bullet filled pockets for a fresh cigar.

The young Mexican paused beside the unholy killer of wanted men and rubbed the back of his neck thoughtfully. He raised a finger and pointed west.

'It is about ten miles in that direction, *señor*,' he replied. 'Running Wolf killed all but one of the escorts and burned the coach. We buried the *vaqueros* close to where they fell. It was a sickening sight.'

Iron Eyes cupped a match to the tip of his cigar

and sucked in smoke as he inspected the tall horse. He stopped and looked over the saddle at the young man.

'You're certain that little Maria was taken alive by the Apaches, boy?' he rasped as he tossed the spent match over his shoulder and rested a bony hand on the saddle horn.

Pablo inhaled deeply. '*Sí, señor*. The surviving *vaquero* told us that he saw Running Wolf hoist her up on to his horse just before he lost consciousness.'

Iron Eyes lifted his thin left leg and poked his boot into the stirrup. In one swift action he had mounted the tall shouldered horse and was gathering in his reins. The bounty hunter did not utter a word as his companion also threw himself up on to his fresh mount.

Pablo adjusted the drawstring of his sombrero and stared at the ghostly rider beside him. He cleared his throat.

'You are very brave, *señor*,' he uttered.

'I ain't brave, sonny,' Iron Eyes argued. 'Running Wolf is a mighty valuable outlaw. I'd be a damn fool not to go hunting his tail.'

Pablo doubted that hunting down Running Wolf for the bounty on his head was the true reason Iron Eyes had accepted this dangerous mission.

'Do you really think my sister is still alive, Señor Iron Eyes?' he asked quietly.

Iron Eyes pulled the cigar from his mouth and

116

blew a line of smoke at the ground between them. His icy stare belied his true emotions as he nodded.

'She's still alive, boy,' he said calmly before turning the horse beneath him to face the gates. 'I feel it in my bones and my bones ain't ever wrong.'

The sentries silently watched as the pair of horse-men thundered out into the moonlit desert. The well-armed onlookers crossed themselves in prayer.

FIFTEEN

Iron Eyes and Pablo had been gone less than ten minutes when Squirrel suddenly awoke from dreams and glanced around the unfamiliar room. For a moment, every sinew of her young body was on edge as she dropped her bare feet off the soft mattress on to the tiled floor of the room. A solitary lantern dimly illuminated the room as she rose and adjusted the new clothing she had been given in exchange for her tattered trail gear. Her small hands flattened the creases out of the itchy material and then moved to the door.

Like all hunters, she moved silently. She pressed her ear at the wooden surface of the door and strained to hear the guard which had prevented her from leaving the room since her arrival.

Sally could not detect any sounds. Not even snoring.

She bit her lip and carefully turned the cast-iron

118

handle before pulling the door toward her. The six-inch gap between the door and the frame was enough for her to poke her head out of to vainly search for the heavily armed *vaquero*.

To her surprise, the corridor was empty.

'That don't figure,' she muttered as she silently made her way out into the candle-lit corridor and on to the top of the stairs. As she tiptoed down its steps, she saw the seated figure of Don Jose sobbing into the palms of his hands.

Squirrel Sally had never seen a grown man weep before.

She stopped and stared at him. She was no longer angry.

The sun had risen as the two riders reached the isolated trail road where the coach had been attacked. Iron Eyes had not spoken since they had departed the hacienda. He had just gripped his reins and chewed on what remained of his spent cigar. As Pablo hauled his reins back to stop his mount, the bounty hunter stared out at the bright surroundings. What remained of the coach was now just a blackened shell of its once highly decorated former self.

There were few clues remaining but the bounty hunter could still read this place like no other.

Iron Eyes dragged back on his long leathers and halted his mount. A cloud of dust spread out from the horse's hoofs as the gaunt figure stared through

119

narrowed eyes at the pitiful sight. A handful of crude markers were dotted around the loose sand where the *vaqueros* had been laid to rest. The dishevelled figure could tell exactly how the escort had been attacked and killed but it was nothing to do with overwhelming numbers. A mere handful of Apaches had achieved this and then taken the young girl with them. Whatever provisions and weaponry the caravan had been carrying had also been taken. The attack had been swift and without mercy.

The Apache were renowned for this. In the mind of Iron Eyes, they had no equal among the various tribes he had had the misfortune of running into over the years.

Running Wolf was said to be the most dangerous of them all. That solitary fact troubled Iron Eyes. He knew that the courageous rebel leader was always two steps ahead of anyone who tried to capture him.

This was not going to be easy, he thought.

Even though he had ridden beside the legendary bounty hunter for hours, Pablo could not understand his ghostly companion. The skeletal figure had said nothing, as though words no longer mattered in his bloody world. Something else was driving him and yet Pablo could not understand what.

Why had Iron Eyes not simply taken the one hundred golden eagles his father had promised him? He could have taken Squirrel Sally and pocketed the cash and returned north. Why had he chosen the far more dangerous option of hunting down Running Wolf?

There was more to the emaciated bounty hunter than met the eye, he thought. Iron Eyes was a mystery which, like his legend, could not be fully understood. Pablo held on to his long leathers and watched the deathly man with a mixture of trepidation and awe. Although he admired Iron Eyes, he could not find it in his heart to fully trust him. Every time the bullet coloured eyes looked in his direction, Pablo felt that Iron Eyes might draw his Navy Colts and kill him.

'There is nothing left to give you any clues to where they went, *señor*,' Pablo said. 'The wind has taken everything away. The tracks have gone.'

'I ain't looking for tracks, boy.' The words came as a shock to the youngster. 'I'm figuring out which way they came and went. Apaches don't ride over a rise when they have a valley to ride along.'

Pablo adjusted his sombrero and mopped his brow along his sleeve. He did not know what his comrade meant but would not admit it.

Iron Eyes swung his right leg over the neck of his horse and slid to the ground. He handed his long leathers to Pablo and walked to where the remains of the coach lay strewn across the arid ground.

The bounty hunter studied the blackened timber for a few moments and then turned. His squinting eyes stared out at the hostile terrain as though he

121

could see things that no one else could see. He ran a thumb along his scarred jawline as he stood silently staring out into the heat haze.

'What do you see, Señor Iron Eyes?' Pablo asked from his perch atop his tall mount.

'I see which way they went, sonny,' the lethal bounty hunter muttered before opening the flap of his saddle bags and pulling out a bottle of tequila. He gripped the cork with his teeth and extracted it. Then he slowly turned and moved closer to his mounted companion. Iron Eyes spat the cork at the sand and then lifted the bottle to his lips. When it was empty he tossed the empty vessel over his shoulder.

The young Mexican was baffled. No matter how hard he looked at the surrounding terrain, all he could see was an ocean of sand.

'I do not understand,' Pablo admitted. 'There is nothing to see but sand and Joshua trees. What can you see?'

Iron Eyes scratched his jaw and watched the undergrowth.

'It ain't what you can see, boy,' he said dryly as his piercing eyes glared out into the desolation. 'It's what you don't see that'll kill you.'

The confused Mexican was about to speak when Iron Eyes grabbed hold of his sleeve. As he hauled Pablo from his saddle, a shot rang out and a bullet caught the ornate horn of the youngster's saddle.

Leather exploded as the rifle bullet ripped the large horn off the neck of the saddle.

Pablo hit the sand hard as the bounty hunter crouched like a cougar, getting ready to leap at its prey. He lay on the sand as the bounty hunter drew one of his Navy Colts and pulled back on its hammer. He then stepped over Pablo and raised his arm and fired in one swift action.

With smoke still trailing from the long barrel of his weapon, Iron Eyes advanced in the direction that the rifle shot had come from. As he stared out into the sun-bleached distance, the Mexican scrambled to his feet and hobbled to the side of the eagle-eyed bounty hunter.

'What is going on, Señor Iron Eyes?' Pablo said as he pulled his own weapon from its hand-tooled holster.

Iron Eyes was silent. He raised the gun again and pulled back on its hammer. Whatever it was the infamous bounty hunter was looking at, it was totally invisible to the shaking Mexican.

'I see nothing,' Pablo proclaimed as he frantically looked to where the far taller Iron Eyes was aiming his Colt. 'Who do you see?'

Again, Iron Eyes did not reply.

With cold determination he levelled the gun. His out-stretched arm remained perfectly still. Then without warning, he raised his free hand and pushed Pablo aside, just as a plume of rifle smoke appeared

123

in the distance. Pablo heard the sound of the shot as he hit the ground.

The youngster got to his knees again and was about to protest being knocked off his feet when he noticed the tear in the bounty hunter's sleeve. As he watched the statuesque figure still aiming his gun, he saw blood trailing from the ripped fabric. The bright crimson that dripped from his knuckles was in total contrast to the dust that covered the bounty hunter.

'You are wounded, *señor*.' Pablo gasped as he struggled to get up off his knees.

'Stay down, Pablo,' Iron Eyes said without looking at his companion. 'I ain't gonna save your bacon a third time. Stay there and hush the hell up. I'm concentrating.'

Pablo remained exactly where he was and watched the strange ghost-like creature who towered above him in startled awe. Iron Eyes held his gun at arm's length as he fixed his attention on something out there beyond the kindling dry brush. The young Mexican had never seen anything like it before. There seemed to be no acknowledgement of his own wound in his maimed face. There was only a gritty determination to place his second bullet into the rifleman and, like all hunters, Iron Eyes was prepared to wait for as long as it took.

Iron Eyes stared across the arid terrain with unblinking eyes. He was like an eagle on a high thermal watching for the slightest hint as to where its next meal was hiding. For what seemed like an eternity, the motionless bounty hunter waited for the merest glimpse of his target.

Then he caught sight of movement behind a scattering of undergrowth. Faster than most men could spit, Iron Eyes stepped to his side and fired.

The desert resounded to the explosive noise of his gun hammer hitting the metal casing of the chambered bullet. A plume of smoke encircled the fiery flash that erupted from the gun barrel. At the exact same moment, Iron Eyes felt the heat of a rifle bullet as it passed within inches of his face.

A muffled groan came from out in the distance yet the echoing of gunfire drowned it out to all but Iron Eyes. He knew that he had claimed the life of the rifleman even if he could not actually see his handiwork.

'That'll teach the bastard it don't pay to shoot at Iron Eyes,' he mumbled. There was no sense of triumph in his voice.

Pablo watched as Iron Eyes slowly lowered his smoking Navy Colt and pulled the hot casing from its chamber. No sooner had the spent casing hit the sand than the tall bounty hunter replaced it with another fresh bullet from his deep coat pockets.

'You have killed him, *señor*?'

'Sure I did,' Iron Eyes replied.

As the thunderous noise of the echoing gunshots faded into the dry desert air, Iron Eyes pushed the barrel of his weapon into his belt and looked down at Pablo.

'What you doing down there, boy?' he drawled as he started walking toward the place he had sent his deadly bullet. 'You can get up now. He's dead.'

Pablo Fernandez hurriedly got to his feet and ran after the long-legged bounty hunter. It was like a hound following its master. Although he was winded, Pablo still managed to chase his emotionless cohort.

'Who is dead, Señor Iron Eyes?' he asked as he drew level with the taller man. 'Who was shooting at us?'

Iron Eyes stepped over some desert brambles and then kicked the rifle toward his companion. He said nothing as he stared down at the body of the Apache. Then he quickly knelt and grabbed hold of the long hair and pulled it clear of the dry brush. His eyes studied the face of the dead Indian and then dropped it.

'Looks like one of Running Wolf's boys,' Iron Eyes said before straightening up to his full height. He glanced around and then spotted a white pony in a gulley. The lean animal looked as though it had never had a square meal but its decorated mane sported carefully woven coloured braid. 'Go get that pony, sonny. It might come in useful.'

Pablo looked totally baffled. 'I do not understand. Why was this Indian waiting here? Why did he shoot at us?'

126

Iron Eyes looked at Pablo. 'Running Wolf told him to kill anyone who showed up, sonny. That's why. Don't ask me to figure out the thinking of Apaches. Hell, I ain't managed to work out why white folks do what they do yet.'

Pablo holstered his gun and ran down the sandy slope to the tethered horse. He pulled its rope bridle and reins free of where it was secured and started to bring the sorrowful animal to where Iron Eyes stood waiting.

'How can you be sure that this Apache is one of Running Wolf's followers, Señor Iron Eyes?' he asked as he reached the bleeding bounty hunter.

Iron Eyes gritted his teeth and then reached down and grabbed the dead Indian's long hair again. He dragged the skinny corpse off the sand and twisted it around.

'Look at his neck,' he growled.

Pablo looked at a scar on the brave's neck. It was a half-moon shaped scar. The young Mexican pulled back as he focused not only on the scar but the bullet hole in the temple.

'What does that scar mean?' he asked.

Iron Eyes released his grip. The body crumpled at his boots as the lean man wiped the palms of his hands down his blood-stained coat.

'A half-moon scar is Running Wolf's mark,' Iron Eyes replied as he turned and headed back to where they had left their own horses. 'If you wanna be one of Running Wolf's rebels, that's the price you gotta pay, sonny. He brands his men like folks brand their cattle.'

The two very different men started back to the dusty road and their mounts. Pablo led the pony as Iron Eyes walked silently ahead of him. There was a brooding in the bounty hunter that unnerved the Mexican. It was as though Iron Eyes knew what the future had in store for him and was resigned to accept it. Even if it meant his own death, he was determined to continue on after the elusive Running Wolf.

Pablo swallowed hard as they reached the pair of thoroughbreds. He tied the pony to his cantle and then stared at the grim-faced Iron Eyes.

Iron Eyes pulled out another bottle from his saddle bags and started to down its clear liquor. When the fumes had filled his flared nostrils, he handed the bottle to the young Mexican. His cold stare watched as Pablo took a few sips and then returned it to the bounty hunter.

'Gracious, *señor*.' He coughed as the lean figure returned the bottle to the satchel. He could see a glint in the lifeless eyes as Iron Eyes patted himself down and continued to glare out at the sun-baked land.

'Does this mean something to you?' he asked.

'It sure does,' Iron Eyes retorted as he located a cigar and placed it between his teeth. 'It means that

128

Running Wolf's camp is closer than we figured. That Apache didn't ride far on that pony.'

A smile came to Pablo's face. 'You mean that Maria might be closer than we dared to think possible, *señor*?'

Iron Eyes struck a match and raised it to the tip of the cigar. He inhaled the smoke a few times and then tossed the match aside.

'She's real close, sonny.' He nodded.

Pablo was about to shout in joy when he noticed the blood dripping from the sleeve of Iron Eyes's left arm. There was concern in his face as he moved closer to the torn sleeve and went to touch it. Before his hands even got close, Iron Eyes pulled away.

'You are bleeding very badly, my friend,' he said.

Iron Eyes glanced into his companion's eyes. 'Fix a fire and rustle up some grub, sonny. I'll tend to this scratch myself.'

The surprised Mexican looked at the bounty hunter. 'We are not going back to the hacienda to get the rest of my father's *vaqueros*?'

Iron Eyes sucked smoke into his lungs and savoured its flavour as he looked at his companion. His hooded eyes remained fixed upon the nervous Mexican.

'You ain't scared, are you?' he hissed.

Pablo shrugged. 'I am not nervous, *señor*. I am just not foolhardy. We do not know how many followers Running Wolf has. We have to get my father's men to help us.'

'Nope. There ain't time to get reinforcements, sonny,' Iron Eyes said bluntly. 'We're going to find his camp on our lonesome, but if you wanna head off for your pappy's hacienda, get going.'

Pablo frowned. 'You would go on your own?'

Iron Eyes blew smoke across the distance between them and nodded. 'Yep. Running Wolf and his army of cutthroats wouldn't figure on anyone attacking them on their lonesome, would he?'

The young Mexican stared at the tall haunting figure with a mixture of admiration and disbelief etched across his handsome features. He could not understand how anyone could face death so willingly.

'Is it possible for us to rescue little Maria on our own, Señor Iron Eyes?' he gulped.

Iron Eyes forced a grin. 'We'll find that out soon enough, sonny. The worst that can happen to us is we'll get ourselves killed.'

'Killed?'

Iron Eyes pulled the cigar from his teeth and nodded firmly at the younger man. His hollow eyes looked at his hand and the blood that covered it. Blood was still flowing freely from his arm.

'Listen up, Pablo. We ain't got time to muster up an army to help us,' he drawled as smoke filtered through his teeth. 'It'd take too long to head back to your pappy and return here. We gotta act now. Besides, Maria ain't got time to wait much longer.'

Pablo thought about his sister.

'You are right,' he conceded.

Iron Eyes sucked the last of his cigar's smoke into his emaciated body and leaned over his companion.

'Get some kindling and start that fire,' he whispered as he glared at his hand. 'You got vittles to cook and I gotta stop this damn bleeding.'

SIXTEEN

The smoke from the campfire rose up into the blue sky as Iron Eyes sat cross-legged beside its flames and watched his long bladed Bowie knife thrust into the heart of the crackling fire. As Pablo sat opposite the bounty hunter holding his skillet over the flames, he watched his companion silently.

Iron Eyes had removed his coat and tore his shirt sleeve away from the deep graze. Blood still flowed from the three-inch-long wound as Iron Eyes pulled the cork from the neck of one of the tequila bottles.

He spat the cork at the sand and poured the strong liquor over the wound. His bony right hand thrust the bottle into the soft sand and then reached for the handle of the Bowie knife. He withdrew it from the hot embers and stared briefly at the red hot metal.

Pablo suddenly realized what his companion was going to do and screwed his face up as though he were about to feel the pain himself.

Iron Eyes placed the hot steel against his bleeding wound as the tequila ignited. A flaming flash rose from his already maimed flesh. The flame only lasted a few seconds but it was long enough for the bounty hunter to lose consciousness. He fell backward on to the sand and dropped his knife.

Pablo dropped the skillet on to the fire and got to his feet. He rushed to Iron Eyes and crouched down beside him.

'Señor Iron Eyes,' he shouted as the painfully thin bounty hunter lay on his back. 'Señor Iron Eyes. Are you OK?'

For a few moments the bounty hunter just lay as though he were dead. His bullet coloured eyes remained open as they stared up at the blue sky. Then his chest began to heave and he stared at the concerned Mexican beside him.

'Has it stopped bleeding?' he hissed through gritted teeth.

Pablo glanced at the graze. It had stopped bleeding. The flesh had been soldered by the fiery combination of tequila and fire. He nodded and helped Iron Eyes off his back.

'The wound has stopped bleeding,' he said.

Iron Eyes shook his head and looked at the arm. He reached for the knife and pushed it back into the

133

neck of his boot.

'Good.' He sighed before plucking up the bottle and raising it to his mouth. 'I'd hate to go through that pain and find out that it hadn't worked.'

Pablo watched as Iron Eyes drank half the contents of the bottle before stopping for air. He made his way back to the skillet and removed it from the fire.

'Are you ready to eat?' he asked the dishevelled man. 'The bacon is ready.'

Iron Eyes raised his head and looked through the flames at the youngster. His fingers found a cigar and placed it into the corner of his mouth.

'You eat it.' He sighed before looking at the remaining liquor in the bottle. 'I'll just fill my innards with this liquor and have me a smoke for dessert.'

Pablo carefully picked the greasy bacon from the skillet and started eating. As he chewed he watched Iron Eyes light his cigar and finish the tequila.

'Do you never get drunk, *señor*?' he asked.

Iron Eyes poked his sore arm back into his coat sleeve.

'I never have, sonny,' he replied before forcing his long bony body off the sand until he was standing. He chewed on the cigar and looked down upon the Mexican. 'Hurry up and finish them hog strips. We gotta hit the trail again.'

'*Sí, señor.*' Pablo jumped to his feet and started to

134

douse the fire by scrapping sand over it. He then cooled the skillet with more sand before placing it into one of his saddle-bag's satchels. 'You are OK to ride?'

'Why shouldn't I be?'

'Your arm.' Pablo pointed at the bounty hunter's limb.

Iron Eyes grunted and then strode to the tall horse bearing his livery. He stepped into the stirrup and hoisted himself up on to its back. He gathered up its long leathers and waited for Pablo to mount his own horse.

'You said before that you know where Running Wolf's camp is, *señor*,' Pablo said as he dragged the high-shouldered stallion around to face his comrade. 'Do you really know where we will find little Maria?'

Iron Eyes blew smoke at the air and nodded.

'That dead Apache came from west of here,' he drawled knowingly. 'Someplace between here and that big ocean. A place where the land is stained red from high mesas.'

'How do you know this?' Pablo gasped.

'That Injun was covered in red dust, boy, and so is that pony of his,' Iron Eyes explained through cigar smoke and pointed. 'There ain't no such sand around here but there is over yonder.'

Pablo looked at the pony and then to where they could see the tall jagged spires poking up over the horizon.

'All we gotta do is follow the fresh hoof marks left by that Apache's pony and we'll find out where Running Wolf's encampment is, sonny.' Iron Eyes inhaled smoke and glanced at his dumbfounded companion. 'Savvy?'

'*Sí*. I savvy.' Pablo nodded.

Suddenly, without warning, the bounty hunter lashed the ends of his long leathers across the shoulders of the horse beneath him. The thoroughbred horse sprang into action and started to thunder across the parched terrain toward the stony spires with Pablo in hot pursuit.

The gaunt horseman followed the trail left by the Apache brave as his young apprentice led the Indian pony behind the tail of his own muscular mount.

The merciless sun had not reached its zenith as both horsemen headed deeper into the hostile desert. Then they saw the wall of red rocks before them and the natural stone archway which led into the mysterious valley beyond. To the young Fernandez, this was a place where he had never gone before. He had no idea that it even existed within his father's vast ranch.

To Iron Eyes this was just where the pony's hoof tracks led. Another unknown place like the countless others that stretched from sea to sea.

They spurred harder. The closer they got, the more they could smell the tell-tale clues that there was an encampment somewhere close.

They did not know it but they were heading straight for Devil's Cradle and directly into the jaws of Hell itself.

SEVENTEEN

A steely determination filled the unholy horseman as he continued to thrust his bloody spurs into the flanks of his mount. As though attempting to run from the constant pain the bounty hunter was inflicting upon it, the thoroughbred horse ran faster than it had ever done before. Iron Eyes whipped the long tails of his reins across the horse's muscular shoulders and encouraged the lathered-up animal to reach the top of a dusty ridge.

The sight which greeted Iron Eyes was unlike anything he had ever seen before. He drew rein and stopped his mount as his bullet coloured eyes focused upon the scarlet wall of rocks. It was massive and rose defiantly out of the desert sand.

Iron Eyes held his exhausted mount in check as his eyes scanned it, looking for any hint of an entrance to what he knew lay beyond its seemingly impenetrable walls. Towering spires, the colour of

138

blood rose up into the sky like devilish fingers.

A stretch of desert sand lay between the ridge where the bounty hunter was perched and the escarpment. It was no more than 200 yards distance to the rocks but Iron Eyes could not see any protective cover. The smooth yellow sand was devoid of vegetation. He knew that it would be suicidal to try and cross the sand unless he could come up with a plan.

His cruel eyes noted the hoof imprints left by the dead Apache's pony in its otherwise pristine sand. They led straight to the stony archway.

Then the sound of his companion's flagging mount drew his attention as it followed the bounty hunter up to the top of the ridge. Iron Eyes glanced over his wide shoulder and stared at the sight of the snorting horse and pony and their equally spent rider.

'You sure took your time getting here,' Iron Eyes growled before returning his attention to the sun-drenched rocks across the sand.

Wearily, Pablo slowed to a halt and watched Iron Eyes rise up in his saddle and balance in his stirrups. The bounty hunter's sharp eyes studied the crimson escarpment again.

'Why did you stop, Señor Iron Eyes?' Pablo asked as he pointed ahead of them. 'The tracks are quite clear. They lead across the sand.'

There was an eerie silence as the skeletal figure

slowly sat down upon his ornate saddle. Iron Eyes said nothing as he reached back and pulled a bottle of tequila from his saddle bags with his bony hand.

Pablo drew alongside the hideous bounty hunter. There was something about the scarred Iron Eyes which the younger horseman admired. He did not know what it was, but Iron Eyes was probably the most honest man he had ever encountered.

The young Mexican watched as the bounty hunter's hands pulled the cork from the bottle neck and raised the glass vessel to his lips and drank. When Iron Eyes lowered the bottle Pablo spoke.

'What is wrong, *señor?*' he asked.

Iron Eyes glanced at Pablo and then returned his narrowed eyes to the red rocks ahead of them. He pointed the bottle to where the stony archway loomed.

'That's the way in,' he declared.

Pablo looked but could not see what the bounty hunter had already spotted. The secret entrance to Devil's Cradle had been well disguised by nature over the countless centuries it had existed.

'I see nothing but red rocks.' He shrugged. 'What do you see?'

Iron Eyes returned the cork to the neck of the bottle and then returned it to his saddle bags. He dried his mouth with the back of his sleeve and leaned toward the Mexican.

'I see shadows, boy,' he whispered. 'Shadows

140

where there shouldn't be any shadows. That means that there's a way into them rocks. You can't see it from here but it's there OK. Mark my words, that's the way into them rocks.'

'You mean the camp we seek is beyond that halo of rock?'

Iron Eyes gave a nod of his head and then looked heavenward at the still high sun. He bit his lip and shook his head. Getting close to the escarpment was not going to be easy, he thought.

'I do not see any sentries guarding the hidden entrance to Running Wolf's lair.' Pablo ventured. 'We could ride straight there without any trouble.'

'And get ourselves shot off our saddles,' Iron Eyes added.

Pablo frowned. 'But there are no sentries.'

'There ain't none that we can see, boy,' the bounty hunter corrected. 'That don't mean they ain't up in them rocks someplace. We're dealing with Apaches. They're tricky critters.'

Pablo looked again at the blood-coloured rocks and vainly searched its crevices for signs of hidden Apache rebels. He could tell that Iron Eyes was trying to formulate a plan of action. Just like him, the bounty hunter wanted to dash across the small expanse of sand to the rocks and rescue little Maria. But unlike the youthful Mexican, Iron Eyes was sea- soned enough to know that it was far wiser to think before acting.

'I just wanna get my hands on them Apaches and rescue that little gal,' Iron Eyes growled as he looped his leg over the neck of his horse and slid down on to the sandy ridge. 'They're over there, boy. Damn it all. They're so close I can smell them.'

Pablo dismounted beside the far taller bounty hunter and tied his long leathers to some brush. He watched as the bony figure paced around the area like a caged cougar until he reached the Indian pony. Then for some reason, he stopped and stared at the animal.

'I knew there was a reason why we brought this little Injun pony along with us, sonny.' Iron Eyes sighed as he ran a hand along the back of the skittish animal.

There was a look of astonishment on Pablo's face. 'What are you thinking, *señor*? What use could that little horse be to us?'

Iron Eyes looked at the younger man and smiled.

'I've just figured out a plan, boy,' he hissed. 'A mighty daring plan but if it works, we'll get into them rocks without being riddled with bullets.'

Pablo looked at the pony and then the emaciated bounty hunter in turn. No matter how hard he tried, he could not think how Iron Eyes imagined the Apache mount might assist them in this dangerous venture.

'How can this skinny pony get us into Running Wolf's stronghold, Señor Iron Eyes?' he asked.

142

Iron Eyes tilted his head. His mane of long black hair fell over his horrendous features. 'You have to be as crazy as a fox to outsmart one.'

The Mexican shook his head. He was no wiser. He was about to probe even deeper when Iron Eyes pulled off his trail coat and hung it over his saddle. As the painfully lean bounty hunter removed his tattered shirt, Pablo moved closer to him.

'What are you doing, Señor Iron Eyes?' he asked as the thin man tossed what was left of his blood-stained short on top of his coat. 'Why are you undressing?'

Iron Eyes paused for a moment and stared at his comrade through his long limp hair.

'Hell, Pablo boy,' he muttered. 'Ain't it obvious? I'm gonna save that little sister of yours.'

EIGHTEEN

It had taken less than five minutes to transform himself into what appeared at first glance, an Apache. Iron Eyes had smeared his brutally scarred torso with a mixture of water and the red dust that was covering the legs of the Indian pony to mask his pale flesh. He then tore his shirt apart and wrapped a strip of it around his mane of long hair.

'How'd I look?' he asked the youngster.

'You look like an Apache, *señor.*'

'Good.' Iron Eyes nodded and then carefully poked his Navy Colts into his belt. 'Give me your rifle.'

'My rifle?'

Iron Eyes nodded firmly. 'I gotta look like that dead Injun. He had a carbine.'

'What are you intending doing, *señor?*' Pablo already knew the answer to his question but still needed to hear the bounty hunter say it out loud.

144

'Why are you pretending to be one of Running Wolf's rebels?'

The long-legged man strode to the younger man and loomed over him. He leaned over until his lips were close to Pablo's right ear.

'I'm gonna ride across the sand pretending to be the same critter that left their encampment earlier, boy,' he drawled. 'I need you to pretend to be dead. I want them to think that one of their braves has killed you and is bringing the body back to show Running Wolf. Savvy?'

Pablo's eyes widened.

'You want me to pretend to be dead?' he repeated.

'I sure do,' Iron Eyes confirmed. 'It'll be mighty risky, though. We could both get peppered with lead if'n they see through our trick.'

'How will I pretend to be dead, *señor*?' Pablo croaked.

'You'll be lying over that high shouldered horse,' Iron Eyes stated. 'And I'll be on the pony. I'll be leading you across the sand. If I follow the tracks I'll locate the way into their camp real easy.'

Pablo thought about his sister and nodded. 'It is a good plan. What happens when we get to the encampment?'

Iron Eyes shrugged. 'We'll either be dead or we'll be ready to start fighting.'

Pablo gave a nervous nod and watched as Iron Eyes secured his own mount to the entangled undergrowth

145

before turning to the other two horses. He paced around the far smaller pony and patted it with his bony hand.

'We'll leave my horse here, sonny,' the skinny figure said as Pablo carefully pulled himself up on to the saddle. He lay across the saddle and gripped his pistol in his hand.

'I hope I do not fall off,' Pablo said as his head hung close to one of the stirrups. 'I have never ridden a horse on my belly before. It is not comfort-able.'

'Just keep that gun hid, boy,' Iron Eyes said as he mounted the bareback pony and gathered up the crude rope reins. He pulled the long leathers of the stallion free and then tapped his boots against the sides of the Apache pony. 'If you feel like you're gonna fall off, just grip on to the fender and remember what's at stake.'

'*Sí*, I understand,' Pablo said as he felt the tall stallion start to follow the smaller pony.

They headed slowly down the ridge toward the desert sand. With his mane of black hair flapping like the wings of a bat, Iron Eyes sat slumped across the back of the pony beneath him as the animals reached level ground. His unblinking eyes peered out from behind the veil of long strands of hair in search of the enemies he knew were watching him. With every stride of the horses' legs, both men felt their hearts quicken.

They were getting closer to the red monolith. Closer to the bullets they felt sure would soon rain down upon them.

Just as Iron Eyes had surmised, there were watchful eyes in the scarlet rocks keeping guard of Running Wolf's hidden valley. A pair of Apache warriors moved through the rocks, unseen by anyone who dared look up into the craggy heights. They had spotted the two horses as soon as they dared cross the unprotected desert sand. The braves recognized the painted pony easily and mistakenly thought they knew its rider as well. Iron Eyes had the shimmering heat haze to thank for the Apaches' confusion.

Not even the keenest of eyes could focus clearly on anything or anyone as the hot midday air moved above the hot sand. Both braves were curious by the sight of the tall horse with the body across its saddle trailing the pony. Just as the bounty hunter had hoped, they thought that their fellow Apache was bringing back his trophy for the rest of their dwindling numbers to look upon.

Tall thoroughbred horses were valuable, even to the Apaches who knew they could easily trade a fine animal for guns and ammunition.

By the time Iron Eyes had reached the halfway point, one of the warriors had started to make his way back down from their perilous perches. He would inform Running Wolf while the remaining

147

brave moved like a sure-footed mountain goat across the high rocks with his carbine in his hand. Iron Eyes lifted his chin off his chest and watched the agile rebel as he gradually descended the crimson rocks.

'We've bin spotted, Pablo,' he hissed through gritted teeth. 'One brave is making his way down to greet us.'

Iron Eyes continued to approach the blood red rock face with the stock of the Winchester resting upon his thigh. A trail of sweat ran down his scarred features. For the first time in his life Iron Eyes realized that he was about to face an untold number of foes.

There was no way of knowing how many warriors lay beyond the towering monolith. How many Apaches were willing to fight to the death for their rebel leader?

Every instinct told him it was a bad idea riding into the heart of the Indian stronghold but the photographic image he had seen in Don Jose's parlour kept him moving forward. The face of little Maria was branded into his mind and he was going to try and rescue her, whatever it cost. His half-naked body bore the scars of every battle he had waged. Iron Eyes knew that if he got too close to the athletic Apache, his deception would be unmasked. Yet if he fired one of his Navy Colts before he reached the camp, the echoing sound would alert Running Wolf that trouble was close.

148

Iron Eyes would have to kill the approaching Indian quickly and silently if he were to gain entry into the hidden stronghold. His narrowed eyes glanced down at the hilt of his Bowie knife in the neck of his mule-eared boot.

Once again he looked at the brave as he leapt from one boulder to the next on his way down to greet him. Iron Eyes knew that it was only a matter of time before he was exposed as an imposter. The closer he guided the pony to the stone archway, the more likely it was that the Apache warrior would realize that he was not who he alluded to be.

The blazing sunlight danced along the barrel of the carbine in the warrior's grip. If he fired that rifle to warn Running Wolf and his men, the game was over.

'Keep that gun cocked, sonny,' the bounty hunter told Pablo as he leaned backwards and pulled the long leathers so that the stallion drew level with the pony. 'One of Running Wolf's braves is making his way down here.'

Pablo had never felt so sick in all his life. Draped like a sack of flour over the saddle bowl and bouncing up and down on his stomach was agonizing to anyone apart from a real dead body. Even so, he managed to whisper his reply back to the ruthless rider masquerading as an Apache.

'My pistol is ready, *señor*.' He groaned. 'I wait for your orders.'

149

Iron Eyes patted the rump of his fellow daredevil.

'Good boy. When I give you the order you sit up and start shooting.' Never taking his eyes off the Apache as he made his way down the crimson escarpment, Iron Eyes leaned down to his boot and caught hold of the handle of his Bowie knife. His bony fingers encircled its bound handle and slid it out from the neck of his boot.

The Indian pony reached the stone arch as the descending warrior clambered down to a ledge. The Apache was about to jump down to the sun-bleached sand when he noticed something different about the rider straddled over the pony.

The Indian started to shout at the figure he knew was not his fellow brave. Then Iron Eyes looked up as the carbine was swung around and aimed in his direction. His cruelly scarred face stopped the Apache in his tracks. The fearful shock of seeing the haunting face of the infamous bounty hunter staring up at him filled the Indian with terror.

As the Indian hesitated, Iron Eyes mustered every scrap of his strength and threw the knife as fast and accurately as he was able. The long blade buried itself into the chest of the startled brave. The rifle fell from his fingers.

There was a sickening gasp and then the warrior toppled off the ledge. He fell and landed heavily on his back. Dust rose from around the body as the bounty hunter quickly dismounted and crossed the

150

distance between them. Iron Eyes looked all around the prostrate figure and then pulled his knife clear of the bloody chest. He wiped the gore from the blade and returned it to his boot.

Iron Eyes ran back to the pony and leapt like a cougar on to its back. He looked at Pablo.

'Now, Pablo,' he shouted as he looked at the narrow gap in the rocks and instantly realized the elusive entrance to Running Wolf's stronghold.

Pablo dropped off the saddle and caught the Winchester tossed to him by his cohort. He cranked its mechanism and then poked his boot into the closest stirrup. He mounted his tall horse swiftly and looked at his companion.

'What should I do?' he asked as he held his mount in check and watched the bounty hunter turn to face him.

'Don't get killed,' Iron Eyes snarled before driving the Indian pony into the shadows of the secretive entrance into the towering red rocks.

Both horsemen thundered through the shadows toward the valley beyond. The sound of their horses echoed all around them in the confines of the narrow trail. Then both riders could see the blinding light ahead of their mounts.

For a few moments neither Iron Eyes nor Pablo could see anything as they galloped toward the blinding light. Then their eyes focused and could see the unexpectedly lush valley beyond. Before anyone within Devil's Cradle realized what was happening, both horses cleared the mountainous rocks and raced out into the luminous area.

Suddenly they realized that the camp they sought was close to the red rocks. By the time they had time to slow their mounts they were well into the fertile valley. The horses continued racing between well-nourished trees and the permanent structures.

Then Iron Eyes hauled back on his rope reins and stopped the pony as it reached a cluster of trees. The bounty hunter dropped from the back of his mount and pulled both his guns from his belt. He cocked the hammers of his weapons as Pablo reined in and halted his stallion. The young Mexican threw himself from his ornate saddle and raced to the side of the hunched bounty hunter. Pablo gripped his Winchester firmly in his hands.

Suddenly they saw warriors rushing from their teepees toward them. None of the heavily armed Apaches seemed to be able to even imagine anyone entering the isolated camp.

Then they saw the pair of intruders in their midst.

Iron Eyes did not wait for the shooting to erupt from their weapons. He blasted both his guns in turn as he defiantly advanced toward the crude structures. Plumes of fiery venom spewed from his gun barrels.

Every shot found its target.

As the less experienced Pablo carefully fired his rifle at the Apaches, Iron Eyes continued moving toward them. The bounty hunter felt the heat of their rifle bullets pass his crouching form but did not slow his advance.

The sound of terrified screams rang out above the noise of the guns and rifles. Then Iron Eyes's guns ran out of bullets. Being out of ammunition did not dampen his desire to find little Maria, though.

His bony hands juggled the Navy Colts and started using them as clubs. Blow by blow, he finished off the last of Running Wolf's small army and then fell to his knees and started to quickly reload his guns. His skilful hands made short work of shaking spent casings from the smoking chambers and replacing them with fresh bullets.

As he feverishly worked, he spotted a much grander building set close to a fast flowing creek. When one of his guns was loaded he rammed it into his belt and got back to his feet again. Pablo moved close to his mentor and looked around the smoke filled area for more of Running Wolf's followers.

'Have we killed them all?' he said as his shaking hand forced bullets into the smoking Winchester magazine. 'Are there any more?'

Iron Eyes finished reloading the second of his famed weapons and tapped the arm of the younger man.

'Listen, sonny,' the bounty hunter said as he primed his gun in his hand and pointed its barrel at the larger structure, 'I hear me wailing. There are

153

young kids in there.'

Pablo's expression changed. It was as though every ounce of colour had been drained from his handsome face. He too could hear the pathetic cries.

'I hear Maria,' he said as the spine-chilling howl of a hatchet-wielding brave rang out from behind them.

They both spun on their heels and saw the unmistakable Apache leader known as Running Wolf throwing himself through the air at them. Pablo went to cock his rifle but the hand guard jammed.

Iron Eyes pushed the young Mexican into the dust and blasted his Navy Colt into the chest of the Indian. Running Wolf turned in the air as death claimed him.

The Apache crashed into the pile of dead bodies behind the bounty hunter. Iron Eyes flipped his lifeless body over and stared into the face he had seen on several wanted posters.

Pablo struggled back on to his feet. He gazed at the body and then into the expressionless face of the gaunt bounty hunter. He went to speak but once again Iron Eyes was faster to the draw.

'That's Running Wolf, boy,' he said.

'You were so fast,' Pablo said. 'I have never seen anyone so fast with their gun as you.'

Iron Eyes nodded and then looked to the structure less than a hundred yards away from where they stood amid the choking gun smoke and spilling gore.

'Go get little Maria, sonny.' He sighed as his

154

intense stare darted between the dead at their feet.

'By the sound of it, that gal ain't on her lonesome.'

Pablo ran to his sister's sobbing cries.

FINALE

Every eye within the compound of the hacienda watched as the line of horses and Indian ponies headed across the arid sand toward them. Don Jose clenched his hands together as Iron Eyes led the troop of young females into the courtyard with Pablo at his side. Iron Eyes said nothing as he dismounted and stared silently at the elegant nobleman who greeted his daughter and the five other females captured by the notorious Running Wolf. One by one they were helped off the ponies and escorted into the impressive house.

The bounty hunter strode into the large building, grabbed a bottle of whiskey and then returned to the water trough set just outside the hacienda. He sat upon the edge of the stone trough and started to devour the strong liquor as he listened to the joyous commotion behind his wide shoulders.

As the weary bounty hunter rested, he thought

about the feisty Squirrel Sally up in her room. He knew he would have to face her sooner or later, but was in no hurry.

After a while Don Jose walked out as the last rays of the sun bathed the whitewashed structure in its crimson glow. The bounty hunter pulled the bottle from his lips and stared at the smiling man.

'How can I ever thank you, *señor*?' the nobleman asked. 'You have given me the most precious of gifts. You have given me my daughter back.'

'Pablo helped.'

'Pablo said that you left Running Wolf's body back at his secret encampment,' Don Jose said. 'Why? I thought he was very valuable.'

'I didn't wanna scare those little gals.' Iron Eyes took another mouthful of whiskey and then swallowed. 'They were terrified enough after the shooting.'

Don Jose was impressed. 'You put the feelings of my Maria and the other captives before the reward money. I am eternally grateful.'

Iron Eyes shrugged as he lit a cigar and inhaled its smoke. 'Ain't no need for gratitude, Fernandez. Just hand over those one hundred golden eagles you promised me.'

Don Jose looked confused. 'But your woman has the money, Señor Iron Eyes. I gave it to her as she told me.'

Iron Eyes rose up and shook his head.

'So she's got the money up in that fancy room, huh?' he asked as his eyes looked up at the second storey of the hacienda. 'That gal never quits trying to corner me. I'd best go on up there and get my money.'

Again, Don Jose looked confused by the statement.

'No, *señor*. She is not in my hacienda,' he said. 'She has left here with the money.'

'What?' The bounty hunter raised a busted eyebrow as he stared long and hard at the Mexican. 'Are you telling me that Squirrel has my golden eagles and has gone?'

The nobleman nodded. '*Sí, señor*. Your Squirrel Sally had my *vaqueros* hitch up her stagecoach. She then put the money in it and drove off. She said she was headed north back to Texas.'

Iron Eyes could feel his blood starting to boil as it travelled around his bruised and battered body. He paced around Don Jose silently for a few moments and then stopped. His icy stare focused on the older man as Fernandez began to move back into the hacienda.

'When did she leave, Don Jose?' he asked before taking a long draw on his cigar.

'She came down from her room just after you and Pablo headed out,' Don Jose informed Iron Eyes. 'When I explained that you had just left, she seemed very unhappy. I do not think she liked the fact that you did not go to see her before you rode out to rescue my dear Maria.'

'Gracious.' Iron Eyes watched as Don Jose entered the hacienda. The sound of happiness filled the air as he turned and led the tall horse toward the stables.

As he reached the fragrant building, a *vaquero* walked toward him and accepted the reins from the bounty hunter. As the man went to lead the horse into the stables, Iron Eyes cleared his throat and caused the man to stop and look at him.

'Is anything wrong, *señor*?' the *vaquero* wondered.

'Nope,' Iron Eyes replied after downing another gulp of whiskey. 'Take my saddle and bags off this nag and put it on my palomino stallion.'

'You are going somewhere?'

With the cigar gripped between his teeth, Iron Eyes sighed heavily.

'Yep, I sure am,' he said. 'I'm chasing a certain gal on a stagecoach.'

'I understand.' The *vaquero* grinned widely and winked at the bounty hunter. 'You are going after the woman you love. It is so romantic that you would chase your woman to the ends of the earth.'

Iron Eyes shook his head.

'Nope. I'm going after my one hundred golden eagles, friend.' He corrected. 'Squirrel's gonna get her rump kicked when I catch that thieving female.'